THE
DETECTIVE'S
NEMESIS

Paperback ISBN: 978-1-80424-162-2
Epub ISBN: 978-1-80424-163-9
PDF ISBN: 978-1-80424-164-6

Published by Orange Pip Books
335 Princess Park Manor, Royal Drive,
London, N11 3GX
www.orangepipbooks.com

HOLMES & CO. MYSTERIES

COLLECTION ONE

Some people's affability is more deadly than the violence of coarser souls.

-Sherlock Holmes, *The Illustrious Client*

Chapter I

The British Government Visits Baker Street

Irene Holmes sat on the carpeted floor of 221B Baker Street staring at the coloured paper in front of her. The fireplace was dwindling from the morning fire. She needed another cup of tea, but focused on the task at hand instead. Grabbing a red paper strip, she looped it through a green hoop, gluing the ends together. The paper chain stretched on for miles; she'd been at this particular project since Joe left early this morning to run some errands before the rain came on.

The chain draped over the couch behind her, past the fireplace, across Joe's desk, then bridged to Irene's own workstation before returning to her.

She wasn't in a particularly good mood today and thought that creating something to decorate the flat would help, but her spirit seemed to grow fouler with each loop.

"Irene!"

Dr. Joe Watson called to her from the bottom of the exactly seventeen steps that led to down to the apartment building's front door. She grabbed a red loop, sticking it through a green one. Why should she move when Joe would be up in a moment and see her sitting here?

"Irene, are you there?"

She rolled her eyes. There was nowhere else to go and nothing else to do. If her flatmate and colleague hurried up the steps, he'd realize that.

There was grunting from the bottom of the stairs, as if Joe were struggling with something. Odd. He never mentioned bringing anything large or heavy home.

Irene paused her craft and listened for a moment, counting each step as the man stumbled up. She twisted her body to look through the flat's open door and into the hall.

Joe turned the corner, out of breath, his winter boots thudding on the carpet. His eyes widened when he spotted her.

"You *are* here!" He paused at the open door and pulled his boots off. "Why didn't you answer me?"

Irene shrugged and fiddled with the paper chain. "I knew you were coming up here eventually and would speak with me

8

then."

"I suppose, but I needed your help..." Joe trailed off, his eyes following the garland as he stepped into the room. "Is this what you've been doing all morning? It is long enough to wrap around the flat at least three times. Where did you get all of this paper?"

She pointed to the large cardboard box next to her, with the label stamped on the front.

"You stole this from the university? Irene..."

She sighed and threw her head back, the garland crinkling as the end flew into the small heap accumulated by her knees.

Joe returned her sigh of dismay with one of exasperation before shrugging off his coat. He tossed it towards the door, followed by his scarf and gloves.

"What's wrong?" he asked, folding his tall bod next to her on the floor.

He smelled of crisp winter air and pine needles, and Irene wondered for a moment where exactly he'd been all morning.

She glanced at him to observe any small clues, but he hopped up, shaking his head.

"Stop deducing me! I asked you a question. I left you here hours ago and you haven't moved. And you're still in your pyjamas."

Irene grumpily pushed the paper chain with her foot, eliciting a tired groan from her roommate.

She finally looked at him then. Joe stared back at her with those sky-blue eyes of his, waiting for an answer.

He'd recently been to the barber to trim his auburn hair, but the strands were still long enough to brush his ears. His appearance had been on the better side of decent since he'd started seeing Sarah James, the librarian, and that meant frequent grooming trips and shopping with Miss Hudson to pick out some lovely new shirts.

Today, however, he was dressed in his usual shirt and vest, the hem of his trousers damp and muddied. Where had he been – a forest?

Irene stood, focusing on what was gnawing away at her mood. She gestured to their investigations board tucked to the side of the flat.

"It's been weeks and I've heard nothing more."

The mysterious letter from AB that arrived a few weeks prior demanded that Irene keep to herself and stop meddling in other's affairs. It was stuck to the board, surrounded by clues from Irene and Joe's first case regarding the woman with the false accent and ties to some curious coordinates in New York.

Joe stood beside her, gazing at the board. When Irene had first shown him the letter, he'd become instantly worried to the point where she had to get mad and promise not to attempt to actively seek out AB.

He now skimmed it again.

"This still seems like a bit of nonsense to me. An empty threat and a failed attempt to keep you from interfering. Obviously, whoever sent you this hasn't been paying attention to who you are and doesn't know you'd never back down, especially from something like this. Honestly, it also sounds like this AB is a spoiled child throwing a fit after having their block tower knocked down."

Irene nodded, reluctantly agreeing. "It's disappointing. I was quite excited to have a nemesis. Something like that would be unique and interesting."

Joe chuckled as he stuck the letter back to the board. "You make enough enemies during our cases, you certainly don't need a nemesis on top."

Irene chewed her lip as she stared at the board. He was correct, of course, but that didn't make her want for excitement wane in any sort of way.

She felt Joe's eyes on her and he gently squeezed her shoulder. "Is that what's been troubling you today?"

Irene bit her lip too hard and tasted blood. Her partner was becoming more skilled at sussing out her moods. He could tell when underlying troubles were the cause of whatever she was feeling at that moment. Occasionally, this caught her off guard.

Turning from the board, Irene stepped over the garland and flopped onto the couch.

"This will be my first Christmas back at Baker Street since moving out as a child."

Joe sat in his armchair, seemingly ready to listen to every word. "You never came back here for holidays while living on the bee farm?"

Irene shook her head, grabbing a strip of red paper that had made its way onto the couch. "We always had Miss Hudson out to stay with us for Christmas and New Year's. And when I moved back to London, I never returned to Baker Street. Miss Hudson and I would visit the Lestrades and have a festive breakfast with them. I don't even know how to host the bloody holiday."

As a final note, she flung the paper. It twirled in the air before dropping to the floor by her feet.

"It's hardly hosting if it's just us," Joe replied, his voice soft and reassuring. "We'll have a lovely day. Perhaps even go out and have Christmas breakfast as well. The day can be as quiet or as boisterous as you want it to be."

She looked at his kind smile and felt her own lips stretch. "It shall be a good day."

"It shall, indeed." His smile turned to a grin, his eyes crinkling.

Just then, a shrill gasp came from the bottom of the steps. Miss Hudson shouted in her angry Scottish accent.

"What on earth? Joe and Irene come here this instant!"

Irene raised her brow. "What could possibly be wrong with her?"

Joe looked toward the hallway with scrunched eyebrows. "Probably the Christmas tree I left in the middle of the front hall."

*   *   *   *   *

By the time afternoon tea came to Baker Street, Irene and Joe had the tree trimmed to perfection.

The seven-foot evergreen stood on the corner of the flat, next to Irene's desk. Shiny baubles and candy canes hung on the

13

boughs, with bits of sparkling angel hair dispersed throughout.

The lengthy red and green paper garland started in the small kitchenette and hung in swoops all around the flat's outer edge, passing Irene's bedroom door, bordering the sitting area, and back past the front door, looping back into the kitchenette.

Irene stood by the Christmas tree, sipping her last bit of tea. She moved angel hair from one spot to another, dispersing the silver strands evenly..

Meanwhile, Joe sat at his desk, scribbling away at a batch of Christmas cards to send to his family.

The front doorbell rang.

Irene and Joe exchanged curious glances with each other. Neither was expecting a visitor and they'd both decided not to chase after cases unless a particularly intriguing one fell across their laps – they'd received enough money from their previous mystery to get them through to the new year.

Miss Hudson's muffled voice drifted up the stairs, then her feet tapped up each step, in a hurry to get to the flat. She swung open the door and swept her eyes over the sitting area, presumably assuring it was neat and tidy.

"Who's here, Miss Hudson?" Irene asked.

"A man from the government," the old woman whispered.

14

"Finally! You may show him upstairs."

As the man entered the sitting room, Irene stepped forward to greet him.

With black hair perfectly parted and slicked back, he looked like an American movie star right down to the dimples in his cheeks. The suit he wore was tailored and his clean-shaven jawline was square and bold. His blue eyes could rival Joe's for sparkle and curiosity.

For a moment, Irene was taken aback by his looks, part of her instantly distrusting such a polished man.

Whenever she visited her Uncle Mycroft, the rooms at the government building were full of stuffy old men who would raise their eyebrow in disapproval whenever she scampered by. This individual, however, looked like he would do most of the scampering himself.

"Basil Cullens," he greeted with an Irish accent.

"Irene Holmes," she shook his hand, then motioned to the couch. "Please, sit."

She took up her own spot on the armrest of Joe's chair.

In turn, Joe quickly introduced himself before sitting beside her on the cushion.

Irene studied Mr. Cullens once again in hopes to deduce

15

anything more about him. A small grey feather was stuck to his trousers, indicating that he perhaps had a bird at home or was involved with the homing pigeons, which was more likely given his government position. There was a large scar on the side of his hand, as if a chunk was blown off at some point at least four or five years ago. His knuckles were scarred, too, perhaps from boxing.

"Miss Holmes." The man spoke warmly as if pleased with Irene's demeanour. "You were quite adamant that we investigate your mysterious woman."

"I was as adamant as I needed to be. Please tell me what you found in New York."

He hesitated for a moment, seemingly surprised by her forward attitude.

"The co-ordinates you gave us led to a joint effort between the American and British government and we found quite the gathering of Nazi sympathizers at that location. The Americans quickly disbanded them and, unfortunately, found no trace of this mystery woman. Other than her involvement with your case, she seems to have no other ties to this group at all."

"I believe she's finished with them," Irene explained, already ten steps ahead of Mr. Cullens. "I assume you read the letter I wrote about the Russian thief we arrested a few weeks ago?"

"I did," the government official nodded. "I will admit, this woman is eluding us and it's quite vexing. We have, however, received word that there is a possible threat to a particular family that's quite important."

"What kind of threat?" Irene perked up.

"Have you heard of the Astons, Miss Holmes?"

She furrowed her brow in an attempt to recall the name. "Do they own a shop?"

Mr. Cullens let out a small chuckle. "They own Aston's Department Store and are one of the oldest and wealthiest families in London."

Irene groaned, dropping her head back, instantly recoiling at the thought of yet another affluent family.

At Mr. Cullens' raised eyebrow, Joe stumbled through an explanation. "We just finished a case dealing with wealthy clients."

"I see." Cullens replied, but the bemused smirk stayed on his lips. "Well, then this will only add to your reputation."

Irene stood and paced in front of the fireplace, ready to hear the story, despite her trepidation with the wealthy. "Tell me why you're investigating this family."

"Mr. Aston died in the forty-four bombings," Mr. Cullens began. "He left the entire fortune and the store in the care of his only son, Timothy Aston, who is set to get married shortly, just before Christmas. We have good reason to believe something may happen at this wedding."

"Why do you believe that?" Joe asked, scribbling down the man's words in his notebook.

"Someone has already taken a shot at the boy. In late summer, as he rode his horse on a hunt in the back lawn. Timothy remained unscathed, but the shooter was never caught. There is also talk about his bride and how fast the marriage is progressing."

Joe nodded. Irene's gaze bounced between the two men.

"Marriages tend to happen fast these days," Joe said.

"They do," Mr. Cullens agreed. "And we have no reason to suspect the bride of any wrongdoing, but the shareholders are concerned that Timothy is going to run the business into the ground as he is the only one with control. Until he decides to pass it on to the manager of the store, he is a wild card."

Irene chuckled. "Shareholders don't like wildcards."

"They do not," the man nodded. "There's no love lost

between the store's acting manager and Timothy. Enough to raise some suspicion toward the manager."

Irene stared at Basil, attempting to discern exactly what he was here to request. "I am confused, Mr. Cullens. What is it that you want *me* to do?"

"I need you to go to the estate," he said. "Interview everyone and search the house and grounds for any indication of foul play or any potential threats that would take place during the wedding. We'll be there for the ceremony to ensure everything progresses smoothly and quell any threats you find."

Joe paused his writing and glanced up at his partner. In turn, Irene folded her arms across her chest, feeling severely disappointed at this entire scenario – especially if Mr. Cullens was insinuating that she should use her talents for a simple security sweep.

"Let me make sure I have this right: I hand you Nazis and you give me dog-sniffer duty?"

Still sitting in the armrest, Joe let out a small groan of worry.

Mr. Cullens hesitated as if sorting out his next words. "That's a very colourful way of putting it."

"It is the correct way of putting it," she retorted hotly. "Why can't one of your agents do it?"

"We are stretched thin as it is, Miss Holmes," the man explained, his words bordering on pleading. "And we have other leads we're following up on. We simply do not have the resources to put into this particular task if we are to continue investigating your mystery woman."

She gave him an icy look. "Then let *me* continue."

"You are, by doing this job for us. From what we've concluded, this entire scenario has her name written all over it. The assassination attempt. The potential plot against the only heir to a large fortune. A rushed marriage."

This attempt to make the case sound more appealing to Irene fell flat. She pursed her lips together. "But you do not know for certain that she is behind this."

"Unfortunately, we do not," Mr. Cullens sighed. "But if you are taking care of this for us, then we can focus on intelligence from other means to track her."

Irene chewed the inside of her lip as she contemplated this man's words. She had no desire to simply do the government's legwork; the temptation to refuse this case was significant. However, if this had anything to do with AB, then Irene wanted a piece of it – no matter how small.

Mr. Cullens took her silence as hesitation and he stood,

offering her a soft smile. "I never met your Uncle Mycroft or your father, but from what I've read about Sherlock Holmes and the stories from others who worked with Mycroft, they were just as tenacious as one another. I've been told you're gaining quite the reputation for being much of the same."

Irene felt her chest puff with pride at the compliment and tried to overlook the other feelings that came with hearing those names. She hated to admit it, but Cullens had pressed the correct buttons. Sighing, she straightened her shoulders and spoke.

"So, I am to solve a crime before one has even been committed."

Mr. Cullens gave a lopsided smile. "Precisely. Just pursue this task as if someone as clever as you wanted to cause some trouble. How would we prevent that?"

"You wouldn't," she retorted, a sly smirk spreading across her face. The government official returned the grin and took a step toward Irene. "Then it's a good thing we're not chasing you, Miss Holmes."

She stared for another moment, trying to read anything behind his blue eyes. He seemed genuine enough. If he was going to be this personable and co-operative throughout the investigation, Irene would welcome that with open arms.

21

"We'll go to the estate and see what we can find," she decided, turning from him and walking to her desk. She grabbed a business card from a pile made up after their last case. "Is there a way we may contact you?"

Mr. Cullens nodded and pulled out his own card. "This will ring directly to my desk. If I'm unavailable, you may leave a message with whoever answers on my behalf."

Irene gazed down at the card, then nodded to wrap up the conversation.

The man stuck his hat on. "Good evening, Doctor, and to you, Miss Holmes. I look forward to hearing about any discoveries you make."

"We shall keep in touch. Good evening."

He gave her one last smile and left the flat.

As soon as Mr. Cullens was out the front door, Miss Hudson thumped up the steps. She entered the room in an excited tizzy.

"He was certainly a handsome chap. And so charming! I hope you agreed to whatever he asked for."

"I did," Irene replied, fiddling with Mr. Cullens' business card. "But his charm had nothing to do with it."

From behind her, Joe let out an amused grunt. Both women turned to him, and his cheeks instantly reddened.

"He was quite nice," he said, stumbling over his words. "And you seemed to get along with him better than I thought you would."

"He is certainly different from the men I remember meeting during visits at Uncle Mycroft's work," Irene replied, sticking the card to the board. "Hopefully, he will continue to be this amiable throughout."

Miss Hudson made a pleased noise. "Working for the government? Oh, how exciting!"

Irene nodded – more to herself than the old woman – in an attempt to build up the excitement of the case.

"We get to play criminal tomorrow, Miss Hudson." She pivoted to face the room, clasping her hands together.

"I'm not quite sure what that means, dear. But between the government and the few affluent people you've assisted, you do have quite the client list, whether you like it or not. A lot of people who could make your name great."

"My name is great whether people know it or not," Irene stated, feeling the same pride from earlier. "Now, I am getting rather hungry, so if you haven't prepared anything for supper, Joe and I shall treat ourselves to—"

"Oh, heavens," the housekeeper scoffed. "Just because you

23

have all that money saved up doesn't mean you have to spend it. Besides, Joe spends enough on Sarah as it it. There is a pie in the oven as we speak, you cheeky thing. So, wash up."

Irene glanced at her partner, who simply shook his head. The corners of his mouth turned up as he tried to hide his smile.

Miss Hudson scowled at them, then headed for the door.

"Perhaps the next time that young man comes calling," she began, looking directly at Irene, "you could run a brush through your hair or put on slippers that match."

Irene shut the door behind the old woman and the two burst into a fit of giggles as soon as she was gone.

"Hey!" Joe exclaimed through his laughter. "One of those slippers is mine."

Chapter II

A Visit to the Aston Estate

The Aston Estate sat on lovely rolling hills just outside of London, surrounded by a substantial forest, with the grounds separated by a rushing creek.

A steady cold December drizzle followed Joe and Irene as they pulled into the long laneway and parked near the garage. The rain had started last night, just after Mr. Cullens left Baker Street, and showed no signs of letting up.

Joe pulled his coat collar tighter around his neck while he hurried beside Irene up the front steps. As they huddled under the canopy, waiting for someone to answer the door, he looked across the courtyard at the second wing of the house, which was overgrown with dead ivy.

Only in his dreams would he have a house this large. After another sweep of the front garden, Joe shook his head, silently deciding that, even in his dreams, this estate was too large.

An ageing man in a suit finally opened and showed them in. He barely said a word to them, merely using a flick of his wrist to order the maid to take their coats and hats. He escorted the pair to a large sitting room that smelled of polish, murmuring that Mr. Aston would be in momentarily, then left Joe and Irene to gaze around the room. It was apparent that this space was barely used, if ever. Large paintings of vast landscapes adorned the space and a rather impressive coat of arms took up the far wall between two full-length windows.

"This is quite the room," Joe observed, marvelling at the antique chest of drawers topped with statuettes and trinkets.

Irene grunted in agreement, already impatient with how long they'd had to wait for Mr. Aston.

*   *   *   *   *

Almost twenty minutes after they first sat on the fancy couch, there was still no sign of a Mr. Aston.

Irene stood up, sighing with impatience. "I have half a mind to find him and drag him in here."

"Sit down," Joe said in an attempt to ease her mood, but his lips were quirked in amusement. "He probably got lost with how big this house is."

"It is ungainly large, isn't it?" She plunked back down on the couch. "What does one do with all this space, anyway?"

Her partner shrugged. "Fill it with family and servants."

Irene made an unimpressed noise and tapped her foot on the carpeted floor.

A flirty male laugh came from the hallway and the door burst open. Timothy Aston sauntered in without a care in the world, laughing at the giggling maid in the doorway. Finally catching sight of Joe and Irene, he greeted them with a pleasant nod and open arms as if they were all old friends.

"Doctor Watson and Miss Holmes, I presume!"

"Mr. Aston," Irene replied stiffly, extending her hand. "I'd like to get started right away."

Timothy looked Irene up and down, not trying to hide where his eyes paused. "When those stiffs from the government told me they were sending you to do a security sweep, they didn't mention how gorgeous you'd be."

Joe sighed inwardly. This entire scenario was going to end up with Mr. Aston receiving a black eye. He meant to intervene, but Irene was quicker with her retort.

"They told me someone tried to kill you earlier this year. I can't imagine why."

Mr. Aston either didn't catch the sarcasm in her voice or perhaps chose to ignore it. "Someone did, yes. I think it was probably an accident. One of my mates having a laugh."

He sat in the large armchair across from them, crossing his foot over his knee in complete relaxation.

"Which one of your mates would think it's funny to fire a gun at you while on a horse?"

She asked the question rhetorically, but Timothy shrugged.

"I have loads of mates. Could've been any of them, really. I doubt the intention was to hit me in the first place. I heard the bang and a whoosh go by my ear. It was probably just to scare me since the horse I have is greener than a pasture."

Irene sat back and muttered something under her breath, so Joe took over the conversation.

"Where did you serve, Mr. Aston?" The boy was younger than him but would've been in his early to mid-twenties during the war. Joe was curious as to what faction Mr. Aston belonged.

"I didn't," he said, without a hint of shame in his voice. "I was at university."

Joe was genuinely surprised at his answer, as he certainly didn't seem to have the polish or intellect as someone who spent the war years studying higher education. He glanced at Irene, and she raised her brow, her jaw set in disbelief.

"University?" she repeated. "For what?"

"I went to Glasgow for my law degree."

Joe readied his pen. "Why didn't you go into law when you returned to London?"

Timothy hesitated, but Irene was quick to answer for him. "Because you never finished the degree, did you?"

Anger flashed across his face for a brief moment, but he quickly adaped a business stance. "The war took its toll on all of us. It made finishing my degree impossible."

Irene let out an unimpressed noise. Joe cleared his throat, eager to move the conversation along before she fought with Aston even more.

"Were you with someone romantically before the war?" he asked next. "Someone from the university, perhaps?"

"I was, but I left her. Her name was Janine," Timothy replied, but even Joe caught the hesitation in the boy's voice as if he was unsure of the name.

"And why didn't you return to her when you came back to London?"

"I did, for a short while. But you know how it is, Doctor.

29

You get bored and want something fresh and new." Lighting a cigarette, Aston glanced at Irene, his eyes moving up and down, and Joe resisted the urge to snap his fingers in the boy's face. "That's when Bernadette came along."

The doctor usually kept his judgements to himself, but the way Timothy spoke about women – as if they were mere hobbies to try and pass on – rubbed him the wrong way; especially since he was going steady with Sarah and couldn't imagine speaking so heartlessly about their relationship.

"And what's to stop you from getting bored with Bernadette?" Joe asked, failing to keep the distaste from his words.

"I am a man in love now, Doctor," Aston said, words light and airy, yet full of falseness.

Irene gave a small chuckle, drawing the conversation back to her. "Why a winter wedding? I would assume spring or summer is more desirable."

"Bernie wanted marriage as soon as possible."

"Is there a specific reason for that?"

"Not that I know of. I am quite a catch, so perhaps she simply wants to tie me down."

"And that doesn't bother you?" Irene pressed. "Her need to

30

tie you down?"

Mr. Aston shrugged again. "She satisfies almost every need I can think of, which is all us men can really ask for. Eh, Doctor?"

He looked to Joe, who offered nothing but a raised brow.

Irene fidgeted on the couch. Joe knew her patience was running out with this man.

"You run the department store, correct?" she fired.

"I own it," the boy retorted, turning smug. "If you want to talk any sort of business, you'll have to speak with Old Man Grouchy."

Joe began writing the name down, then stopped halfway through. "I assume that's not his real name."

"No. I've been calling him that for years, though."

Irene sighed. "Could we get his actual name, please?"

"Barnes," Aston finally replied, taking a drag from his cigarette. "He's got an office at the store on the fifth floor if you wish to speak to him. Though I don't know why you'd need to."

"Do you not participate in any of the business affairs?" Joe asked as he finished writing.

Aston shrugged again, blowing out smoke. "I mostly sign papers and pass orders. The company practically runs itself; Old Man Grouchy makes sure of it. Father left him everything but the actual company."

"If you have no interest in running a department store, why not just give the company to Mr. Barnes?" Irene inquired.

Timothy scoffed, squishing his cigarette butt in the decorative ashtray atop the accent table beside him.

"I'm not handing anything to that overgrown baboon of a man. He was horrid to me my entire childhood. You know, one time we were in Harrods and my father wouldn't buy me a particular toy. Barnes thought I was disruptive, so he spanked me right there in front of the store. Hauled me over his knee in front of everyone. I've loathed him since. I wouldn't even leave the company to him in my will."

"That must make him fairly upset," Irene observed flatly. "He does all the work and you reap all the rewards."

Mr. Aston waved her off, offering her a lit cigarette. When Irene shook her head, he shrugged.

"I suppose he must be irked, but I barely have any contact with him. I usually go into the offices every other week or so to sign whatever they need me to."

Joe finished jotting down more thoughts. "We will add him to the list of suspicious characters nonetheless."

"Why?" the boy asked. "He has no reason to want me dead."

Irene gave him a sidelong look. "Purely for joyful revenge for years of being a brat and not handing over a company he clearly runs, perhaps?"

Joe immediately intervened, leaning in between them. "We'll wrap this up in a moment. Just one more question. Can you think of anyone who would want to harm you or your bride?"

"Not at all," Aston replied. "I've got plenty of mates and a loving fiancé. Everyone adores me, Doctor."

Joe should've stopped Irene before she said anything more, but he was too slow.

"Is adore the word they'd use?" she quipped.

Mr. Aston pointed the lit cigarette at her, dropping ash to the floor. "You are out of line, Miss. Your gentleman here needs to have a word with you about how to address a man of importance."

"When we come across one, I'm sure he will."

Timothy leaned forward, mouth agape at the apparent gall of a woman speaking to him in such a manner.

Joe needed to end this quickly or they'd be pulled from the case. He stood, gently grabbing his partner's arm and tugging her to her feet.

"We shall speak with Bernadette now. Where can we find her?"

Aston sat back in his chair, clearly finished with the conversation. "In her wing, doing something with dresses or her stitching, I don't know. The housekeeper will show you. Just call for any of them. We've got so many."

"Excellent," Joe said, a little stiffly. "Thank you."

He gave Irene another gentle tug, and they left the sitting room.

*   *   *   *   *

Miss Bernadette Harrington sat amongst several garments in her bedroom's sitting area, already looking nervous and flighty before Joe and Irene even spoke to her. Her mousy hair was pinned away from her sharp face and her frame was slight – as if she'd blow away in a heavy wind.

Irene stayed silent, seemingly deducing the young woman. Joe tried his best as well, but all he saw was a shy person whose eyes darted around the room like someone might sneak up on her at any second.

"Thank you for speaking with us," Irene said finally. "I'm

sure you are rather busy with the upcoming wedding."

Bernadette sighed and stroked a piece of fluffy fabric in front of her. "Very busy, yes. But I will try to help as best I can."

"Much appreciated."

The girl looked back at Irene and grew more nervous with each passing second. Joe couldn't take it any longer and asked a question.

"Can you think of anyone who would want to harm you or Mr. Aston?"

She shook her head. "No one. I thought this was all just a formality. You truly believe that there is someone who might want to harm us?"

Irene glanced at Joe, focusing on something in his hair, before answering Bernadette. "We're not sure, but we've been asked to ensure everyone's safety."

She looked at Joe again, at the same spot on his head. What was she focusing on?

Suddenly self-conscious, he quickly ran his hand through his hair to remove whatever debris lay in the strands. He caught the faintest reaction from Bernadette – a small flinch.

Like the flip of a switch, Irene changed her demeanour and fired questions at the poor woman. "Does Mr. Aston get angry often? Does he try to control you?"

Miss Harrington shook her head. "Goodness, no. If anything, he doesn't take things seriously enough, but he gives me free rein to do whichever I please."

"I see. And your previous husband, did he die in the war?"

The girl's eyes widened. Joe probably shared look of shock as he stared at his partner, searching his mind for a connection as to how Irene made that deduction.

Bernadette was still taken aback, fidgeting even more with the cloth on her lap.

"He didn't die in the war. He... I'm sorry, Miss Holmes, but how did you know I was previously married? It isn't something I tend to share."

"It is quite obvious," she replied. That seemed to put a small bit of fear into Bernadette, but Irene didn't appear to notice. "There is still a scarred indent on your finger where your previous ring sat – as if it were too tight or you spent a lot of time with your fists clenched. You seem weary with the world and have lost the innocence that comes with first loves. Also, and I'm sorry if this offends, but you are of the age to have been married by now."

Joe had no idea where Irene was going with her questions,

so he sat back and let the women speak, jotting down their conversation in his notebook.

"I suppose that is all true," Bernadette mumbled, looking at her feet. "But how did you know Ryan died?"

"Divorce is hardly commonplace. Also, it wouldn't do the Aston reputation well if Timothy married a divorcee, but a widow is a tragic tale that is easy to spin for the presses. And considering there have been no scandals involving your marriage, I can assume that your husband died, and you'd moved on."

"You are quite observant, Miss Holmes."

Joe caught the worry in her voice. This poor woman must have had such a terrible past and was nervous about what Irene would dig up. Understandable, as his partner occasionally lacked the tact to stop herself from deducing someone in insult.

"I am," Irene said. "Did he die in the war?"

Bernadette was still nervous. She grabbed a handful of long hair over her shoulder and played with it as she spoke. "He made it through the war and died in an automobile accident last year. A taxicab hit him."

"I'm sorry to hear that," Joe paused his writing to look at her.

"When did this happen?" Irene asked, her face emotionless and unreadable.

"Last year. In the late fall."

"Did he have any siblings?"

"A brother, Aaron Inglis. I'm not sure what all of this has to do with my wedding."

Irene gave what she probably thought was a reassuring smile, but to Joe it was the smirk of a predator. "Just collecting information to keep everyone as safe as possible."

Miss Harrington didn't seem wholly convinced, but Irene didn't allow her any time to dwell on her thoughts.

"Your future husband seems to like women very much."

Joe finally intervened. Usually, Irene was more delicate in dealing with fragile-appearing women, but it was as if she wanted to garner a reaction from Bernadette or simply didn't care how the woman felt. He knew his partner could be dismissive of others' feelings, but she seemed particularly combative today.

"We do not mean to offend," he offered. "We are simply attempting to gather a bigger picture of each of your lives and how that may affect the security of your upcoming ceremony."

The young woman nodded reluctantly. "Timothy has told me

38

all about his past indiscretions. I know he isn't a perfect person. He has assured me that I am the only woman he looks at and the only one he wants to be with. I love him, and I am excited to marry him."

Irene stood abruptly. "That concludes our questions. If you don't mind, we shall quickly interview the staff."

With those words, she strode out of the room.

Joe scrambled behind her, muttering an apology to Bernadette.

He caught up to Irene as she descended the stairs to the house's lower wing.

"You want to explain to me what that was all about?"

Irene raised a brow while she led him to the back of the house, to the servant wing.

"I don't know what you mean."

"I'm used to your abrupt questions, but you were almost rude to that woman."

She frowned at him, pausing outside of the servant's quarters. "She was only going to tell us so much before it would turn into a script in her head."

"You think she is hiding something?"

Irene put her finger to her lips, motioning for him to be

quiet.

"We shall walk the grounds after these next interviews and discuss it. Fewer ears to hear our words."

*　*　*　*　*

The staff interviews didn't reveal much – at least not to Joe. He scribbled down a few key points, but otherwise, they all said the same things. The younger maids were all smitten with Timothy and his mates, and the older workers claimed he drinks too much; and while a reckless young man, he was otherwise harmless. Timothy was generous with his money, and Bernadette was lovely, though she kept to herself.

All in all, not much to tell, but Joe was anxious to hear his partner's opinions about everyone as soon as they were alone.

*　*　*　*　*

Irene snapped a picture of the small corner in a room on the high second story overlooking the banquet hall.

"You think a sniper would actually set up here?" Joe asked, gazing down at the polished floors and dozens of tables set up around the dance floor's outer sections.

"People who say they are loved by everyone are usually hated by many. If Mr. Aston rubbed *me* the wrong way, think of how many others are annoyed merely by his presence alone."

"Everyone rubs you the wrong way."

She gave him a pointed look, but a smile tugged at her lips. "I wouldn't put it past someone to sneak in here and attempt to take another shot at him. Have you written down the other weak security points?"

Joe nodded, wiggling the notebook in his hand.

"Excellent work," Irene commended him, handing over the camera and bag. "Let's circle the estate from outside, just for a different perspective. Then, I believe our work here is done."

*   *   *   *   *

Irene skipped ahead of Joe, leaping atop a low brick wall surrounding a large, paved garden. She surveyed the rest of the massive lawn, looking past the stables with a hand on her hips.

The scene made Joe smile. He took a photograph of her. While Irene was good at photographing other people, there were no pictures of her anywhere in the flat. He didn't even have one of them together, despite them being best mates.

He wasn't the greatest photographer, which meant the picture would probably turn out blurry. Joe never seemed to have any luck with outdoor photos, but the scene captured his friend perfectly.

Not having noticed, Irene hopped down from the wall. "There is no blatant reason someone would want to harm these two people at this moment. We will obviously look into the assassination attempt on Mr. Aston and certainly Bernadette's abusive ex-husband."

"I made that assumption about the ex-husband as well," Joe frowned. "The way she flinched when I raised my arm unsettled me."

"Which was my purpose for that activity."

He stared at his partner for a moment, then sighed, realizing how he'd been manipulated. "There was nothing in my hair, was there?"

Irene shook her head. "I had already made a small assumption, given her demeanour, and needed to test my theory. I've unfortunately seen many victims of abusive men through Madame Jeannie's house."

"At least Mr. Aston doesn't appear to be so."

"No. An idiot, yes, but not abusive."

She looked back towards the grand forest that led to the river and set her jaw in what Joe knew was determination. He almost groaned out loud. They'd probably be wandering through that forest before this case ended.

Irene spun around and skipped past him, heading for the laneway.

"Come, Joe. We must get back to London. We've got people to investigate and a trip to Scotland Yard to make."

Chapter III

An Argument to Keep the Investigation

Irene and Joe walked down the busy pavement of downtown London, weaving in and out of shoppers and travellers. The row of shops were crowded with people bustling about with bags and boxes.

Snow drifted lightly toward the earth, melting before it even reached the ground. That's how Irene knew it wouldn't last. The weather would warm tomorrow and the rain would fall before people could even remember it had snowed today.

A snowflake landed on her lashes, impeding her vision. She blinked rapidly in an attempt to melt it.

Joe laughed, watching her struggle, reaching out to help. The flake melted before he could brush it away, so instead, he gave her hat a small bop, and they continued walking.

"Mr. Cullens seemed quite taken with you," he observed

with a light chuckle.

"He was trying to convince me to do a menial task for him. He had to charm me."

"No, he didn't. He needed to appeal to your sense of adventure and he could've done that without the winking."

Irene scowled, suddenly embarrassed, and attempted to recall everything she had said to Mr. Cullens, hoping her words didn't make her seem anything less than intelligent.

"His job is to make people do tasks for him. Besides, you heard Miss Hudson. My slippers didn't match and I hadn't washed up yet."

Joe laughed, surprising her. "And yet, he still winked. You deserve someone who is still taken with you, Irene. Even when you are at your most... *you*."

She rolled her eyes. "That was a terrible sentence."

He laughed again and seemed so carefree that his happiness turned contagious. She felt her own mouth tugging into a smile.

A group of children scampered past them, aiming for the same destination: the large department store half a block away.

"London feels normal again," Joe said. "Doesn't it? Or, at least more normal than it's felt in a very long time."

"It does," Irene agreed. "I do hope it snows on Christmas.

45

Even a light falling, like today."

"That's a very romantic thought," her partner teased.

"Christmas should have snow," she stated, her ears growing warm. "We'd get lots of snow out on the farm. I'd gather dyed water and, while my father played his violin, I would paint pictures in the snow, attempting to reproduce Van Gogh and Degas. Before that, when we lived at Baker Street, I'd watch the snow collect on the window ledge and press my finger against the glass, attempting to melt the flakes."

"We can do that again this winter. I've decided to stay in London for the holiday, as I have a reason to this year. I shall celebrate Christmas with you – and my friends and Sarah, of course. I think I've finally convinced my parents to get a telephone; if they do, then I shall ring them on Christmas day. Perhaps we can send them a card with a photo of our decorated flat or of us."

"That sounds brilliant," Irene replied. An unexpected worry stirred in her belly, though.

She hadn't realized that Joe being absent on Christmas was even an option. He wasn't, of course, but the panic was retroactive and intrusive, making her momentarily nauseous.

"I shall write your sister separately," she added, attempting to quell the uneasy feeling. "She seems to enjoy my tales of our cases."

"That would delight her to no end. I also must start my Christmas shopping as I have severally lacked in that department."

"Perhaps you'll find something in the store."

Irene looped her arm through his, relishing the slight warmth from his body as they walked closer to the store.

The group of children that ran past them earlier had stopped at the large display window, gasping and pointing at the pile of toys on the other side of the glass.

The pair paused at the display as well, their reflection staring back. The two of them, arm in arm, tiny flakes of snow dancing around them and melting on their jackets, looked like the front of a Christmas card. It was a lovely picture.

Irene smiled at the image, then looked past the two of them to the display. The small, motorized train wound around a large Christmas tree with shining ornaments hanging from every bough. Dolls and toy guns were propped next to each other, and playing cards and board games were set out as if beckoning someone to sit down and take a turn.

Joe cleared his throat, and she looked up at him. His cheeks were red, but not from the cold. He slowly and gently pulled his arm out as he stared at their reflection.

Irene let him go.

When he took a small step away from her, she realized that he didn't want her arm through his anymore. It made her instantly sad and confused, and the feelings must've shown on her face because Joe immediately offered an explanation.

"I'm sorry, Irene. Sarah has already been so accepting of our friendship and our living situation, and I wouldn't want her to get the wrong idea or think..."

He trailed off as if hoping an explanation would fall from the sky.

Irene clenched her fists as a wave of frustration swept over her.

She didn't like her life being dictated – and that included her friendships. She'd taken a liking to Sarah, if only because the woman seemed to make Joe happy, but now this added presence was changing how she and Joe acted toward each other and Irene didn't appreciate it for one moment.

Joe stared down at his boots. He looked so heartbroken that she swallowed the frustration for his sake until it was nothing but a flicker of mild annoyance.

"Come," she said in an attempt to steer the conversation elsewhere. "Let's hurry into the store before the children run us over."

The inside of Aston's was massive, with people everywhere, talking over each other, sidestepping and peering over top of one another to glean what lay on the shelves and racks.

Irene and Joe found a worker who looked simply overwhelmed that quickly pointed them in the direction of the offices.

They rode the lift, stiff and nervous, and arrived on the fifth floor. Mr. Barnes' office was at the very end of a long hallway, with closed doors lining each wall. A secretary sat outside, sorting through papers and occasionally glancing at a large typewriter.

She looked up as they approached and gave them a sweet smile.

"Hello, there. Can I help you?"

"We're here to see Mr. Barnes," Irene announced, scanning the secretary and picking up any clues in case of need. The woman was unmarried, had a small brown dog, and bit her nails.

"Do you have an appointment?" she asked, flipping through a diary on her desk.

49

"We do not. But we are here as part of an official investigation regarding Mr. Aston. He will want to see us, I assure you."

The secretary raised a brow and looked worried. "Are you solicitors?"

"No. Investigators. Mr. Barnes is not in trouble."

She hesitated briefly before standing. "One moment."

The woman stuck her head in the office behind her and mumbled a few sentences before returning to Irene and Joe.

"Go ahead."

The pair entered the office and the secretary shut the door behind them.

Mr. Barnes was larger than Irene expected; the small desk he sat behind made his belly appear even larger.

"Good afternoon, Mr. Barnes," she strode forward, holding out her hand. "I'm Irene Holmes and this is my colleague, Dr. Watson."

Mr. Barnes grunted as he stood, but shook both their hands with a firm, tight grip.

"You're here about Timothy," he said, gesturing to the two seats across from him. "He in trouble? Wouldn't surprise me."

Irene shook her head. "Not necessarily. We've been tasked

with a small investigation before his upcoming nuptials to ensure the wedding ceremony proceeds without trouble. Were you invited to the wedding?"

The man seemed momentarily taken aback by her boldness, but quickly regained his composure.

"I was not, and yet, Mr. Aston expects me to find funds for the elaborate affair somewhere in our yearly budget."

"What can you tell us about Mr. Aston?" Irene asked. "Also, were you aware someone tried to shoot him?"

Mr. Barnes rolled his eyes. "Yes. He used the incident to draw out a will and make it well known that I was to be completely excluded from the document."

This confirmed what Mr. Aston had remarked. Business politics seemed so petty, especially with a potential threat on the line.

"Curious," she said, glancing at Joe as he continued writing, steadfast as ever. "So, you weren't invited to the wedding, yet had to find funds for it. Not only that but you were excluded from a will despite you running the company with no help from the actual family."

Mr. Barnes eyed her, his suspicion rising. "That is correct."

"That must make you a tad frustrated. Possibly even a little

51

mad?" Irene pressed.

His demeanour didn't change; he still sat like a toad on a log behind his desk, but his cheeks grew red at her words.

"It makes me want to quit my job right on the spot," he grumbled. "But I've put too much blood, sweat, and tears into this company to simply walk away."

"So, you'll continue to endure being second on the totem pole even with all the work you put in?"

He shrugged and shuffled some papers on his desk. "What else is there to do?"

"Seek revenge?" Irene offered. "Attempt to disrupt something that would make Mr. Aston happy?"

Mr. Barnes finally caught on to what she was suggesting and his face reddened even more, the colour seeping into his neck.

"And when would I have time to plan something like that? It's Christmas. Our sales are neck and neck with Harrods. I do not like where this conversation is going and I ask that you take up no more of my time. Goodbye, Miss Holmes."

He dismissed them with a wave of his hand. His secretary must've been listening right outside the room because the door opened and she cleared her throat, catching their attention.

Joe shut his notebook and stood, but Irene remained where

she was.

Mr. Barnes busied himself with papers, completely ignoring her, but the red in his face never lessened.

Irene wanted to delve deeper into the relationship this man had with the Aston family, but she knew she'd outstayed her welcome. If she pushed her luck, both she and Joe would most likely be banned from the department store altogether.

So, instead of causing more of a scene, she stood and dropped her business card on his desk. "Please call if you think of any other information or reasons why something might go wrong at this ceremony. Good day."

*   *   *   *   *

Mrs. Inglis, Bernadette's former sister-in-law, set a tray of tea and dry biscuits on the table in front of the two investigators, then hurried back to the kitchen to let them speak privately to her husband.

Mr. Aaron Inglis sat on the couch across from Irene and Joe, in a sitting room that was a tad too dark, with a radio humming low in the corner. He shifted on the cushions, adjusting himself with his one leg, the other lost to the war.

He'd welcomed Irene and Joe into his home as soon as they

mentioned his brother, seemingly eager to speak with them.

"Are you looking into his accident more?" he asked, lighting a cigarette.

"Sort of," Irene replied, sipping at her tea. "We've been asked to investigate anyone related to Bernadette Harrington and her soon-to-be husband in order to ensure their wedding ceremony runs smoothly."

Aaron nodded in understanding and spoke with a certain melancholy as if saddened by the news that Bernadette had moved on and was presumably happy. "I heard she was marrying into the Aston family. Good for her."

"Your brother was killed by a taxi, correct?"

Aaron nodded. "Made it through the whole bloody war and it was a stupid accident that got him."

"Please don't take offence to my next question," Irene said, and both Joe and Aaron glanced at her warily. "Was there any evidence of foul play?"

"Foul play? Whatever do you mean?"

"Your brother was not the nicest man, from what I've been told. I heard he had quite a temper."

She saw Joe cringe beside her, but kept her focus on Aaron.

The man lowered his head, closing his eyes momentarily.

"The war hit him hard. He was angry at everything and everyone. I didn't know the extent of it until Bernadette ended up in the hospital with two broken ribs. I tried to help him – I promise you I did – but I couldn't. He was my brother, but I could only do so much before abandoning him. And I wasn't going to do that."

"But you don't suspect her?" Irene asked, setting the dry biscuit down and clasping her hands on her crossed legs.

Mr. Inglis shook his head. "I don't think so. She held onto him so tightly and seemed to love him despite what he would do to her."

"That doesn't mean she still wouldn't want him gone." Irene solemnly pictured the bruises and cuts that some of the women from Madame Jeannie's would come away with at the hands of a rough man.

Aaron blinked in shock. That was when Joe quickly intervened.

He'd been saving the interviews quite successfully today. Irene wasn't trying to be combative, but her anger and frustration seemed to bubble at the surface. She was thankful Joe was quick on his feet at soothing conversations.

"This is a rather complex investigation," Joe explained.

"We're just covering everything we can think of so we won't have to bother you again. Now, is there anyone else who'd want to harm your brother? This may be simply an accident, but if we are going to pull the file from Scotland Yard, we want to be confident it's with good cause."

Aaron stared at Joe for a moment. The man must've liked what he heard because he sighed in resignation and answered.

"He was young and had a big mouth, but he never made any enemies. At least none that I knew of."

"Thank you. We will leave you our card. Please telephone if you think of any other information."

Joe pulled their business card from a small flap at the back of his notebook and handed it over.

Mr. Inglis took it, then gave Irene one last look. "When you see Bernadette again, please let her know that I am truly sorry for the hurt my brother caused her."

"We will," Joe promised.

They left the small flat and headed down the street to where their automobile was parked nearly a block away. The sun was setting and the roads were filling with people returning from work.

Irene strode ahead, only half-aware of Joe attempting to

keep up with her. She chewed her lip, trying to connect all the dots popping up in this case.

The doctor finally caught up to her, pulling his coat higher around his neck as a gust of sharp wind whistled past them. "I feel like the more we investigate this family, the more doors we open to various other paths."

"Precisely," Irene replied. "It is both intriguing and excruciating all at once. We take one step forward and two steps back."

"You really think someone in a taxi purposefully hit Ryan Inglis?"

"An abusive husband dies suddenly in a car crash, and a month later, the wife has moved on? There has to be more to uncover – unless Bernadette was ready to move on well before his death."

Irene went to grab her partner's arm as was her habit whenever they walked anywhere, but she stopped herself, holding her arms stiffly at her sides.

"Come." She picked up the pace to keep her mind focused on their destination. "Let's get back to Baker Street. Those biscuits Mrs. Inglis served were dry and tasteless. They made me crave something sweet from Miss Hudson's cupboards."

*　　*　　*　　*　　*

Irene never did get those biscuits from Miss Hudson because as soon as she and Joe entered through the front door, the older woman appeared at the top of the stairs and quickly beckoned them up. She made some wild gestures with her hands, but Irene already knew they had visitors. Heavy footprints on the carpeted stairs told her two men were waiting for them in the flat.

She and Joe hurried up the steps, tossing their coats, hats, and gloves into Miss Hudson's arms.

When they entered the room, Irene instantly recognized Mr. Basil Cullens' broad, square shoulders as he sat on the sofa. An odd smile tugged at her lips.

But any trace of pleasantness fell from her face as she turned her gaze to the mystery man beside him.

They both stood and greeted Irene and Joe, with Mr. Cullens giving a quick introduction for his partner, Mr. Digby.

Within minutes, Joe was in his armchair, and Irene hiked her hip onto the armrest. She stared at the man sitting next to Mr. Cullens, attempting to get some sort of impression from him.

He was older, close to sixty if the deep lines on his face were anything to go by, and he had a permanent false smile on his lips, which grew even broader when he spotted Irene's scowl. She was already on edge, ready to bristle at any change, and a new government agent interfering in the middle of a case was something she did not want to even attempt to tolerate.

"I thought we were dealing with only you, Mr. Cullens? You informed me there were no more men to spare."

"I did say that, Miss Holmes, and I sincerely apologize," he replied. His lips turned down with a frown, and his dark eyebrows pushed together as he glanced at his partner.

"It's my fault, Miss Holmes." Mr. Digby, the intruder in question, tried to reassure her with a smile, but she kept her expression flat. "I had perused the information you provided and thought I would lend a hand. I saw that you'd mentioned Mycroft Holmes in your letters. I worked for him for several years when I was younger. I was quite sad when he passed. His mind was unmatched."

Irene nodded in understanding, but she was still wary. Perhaps it was because Mr. Cullens had put her so much at ease and seemed completely opposite to the government men she was used to.

Mr. Digby, however, was exactly how she remembered them

all. Stuffy, with a false sense of arrogance, merely looking for a compelling case and ready to take all the glory.

Mr. Cullens started the conversation again. "I briefly spoke to Mr. Aston a few hours ago to make sure everything went smoothly. Apparently, you two left quite the impression on him."

"He was insufferable," Irene muttered. "A rich idiot who deserves to be knocked down a peg or two."

The younger agent attempted to hide a smile as he spoke. "I see. Were you able to look past that and search the house?"

"Of course." Her words came out rather defensively. She was a professional, after all, no matter what Timothy Aston said. "There isn't much to tell, I'm afraid. We have photos of where possible snipers could set up. But if there is security at the entrance to the hall and at the side doors, then no one should be able to position themselves as such.

"We could worry about the priest performing the ceremony, but he should be fine if he is well-known or kept watch. There is the potential for foul play with the staff, but they all seem to adore both Mr. Aston and Bernadette."

"Excellent," Mr. Cullens nodded. "I sent you in there blind, and you've produced far more than I expected."

"There is more," Irene puffed out her chest at the praise and the pleased look on the man's face. "In regards to the attempted murder of Mr. Aston in the fall. We interviewed Mr. Barnes, the department store manager and he said that even if Mr. Aston were to die, he wouldn't be receiving anything in the will anyway. Thus, there would be no point in attempting to kill him unless he wanted to exact some desperate revenge – which, judging by the look of him behind that small desk of his, would be unlikely. However, I will continue to look into whoever took a shot at Mr. Aston because it is still highly curious. The death of Bernadette's first husband is also suspect and worth my time as well."

Mr. Digby shook his head, his fake smile finally dissipating. "Don't trouble yourself with those minor cases. They've been closed by Scotland Yard and are inconsequential to this investigation."

Irene gestured around the room, then to herself in a pronounced way. "In case you haven't noticed, Mr. Digby, I am not Scotland Yard. I shall conduct my own investigation into those matters as it is my job."

The older gentleman went to retort, but Mr. Cullens intervened.

"You may look into them if you wish, Miss Holmes, but they have been closed. Scotland Yard investigated the shooting but could find no evidence of anyone in the woods where the shot came from, and the bramble and trees were simply too thick for anyone to hide back there. If they had, they would've left traces for the detective inspectors to find. As for Bernadette's ex-husband: we briefly looked into it, but again, it was closed by Scotland Yard."

Irene nodded but was dissatisfied with his answer. She believed Mr. Cullens was truthful, but she knew she couldn't rest until *she* had put effort into those two mysteries that were, in her mind, becoming more pertinent to this case.

She wanted to argue her point, but had a feeling that if she persisted, then Mr. Digby would order all those particular files pulled from Scotland Yard in an attempt to get her to focus on the case they deemed the most important. Instead, she nodded as if complying with their instructions entirely.

She couldn't pull off the false smile as well as Mr. Digby, but she attempted her best.

"We will keep in touch with any other information pertaining to Bernadette or Timothy."

"Thank you," Mr. Cullens said, his shoulders relaxing with

relief. "We will bid you both good evening."

"Before we go," Mr. Digby added quickly. Irene gritted her teeth to stop the cuss word from escaping her mouth. She was done with the government for today and was eager to get to supper and progress with this case. "May I have one of your business cards?"

"I've already got one," Mr. Cullens said, patting his jacket pocket.

It gave Irene a small sense of pride knowing someone like him carried around her card.

"I'd still like one for myself," Digby argued.

"It's no trouble," Joe said, handing it to him.

The man spent a second too long staring at the card before tucking it into his pocket, then nodded goodbye at them both. Mr. Cullens followed him out of the flat but paused at the door.

He looked at Irene, his blue eyes and dimples in full force.

"Thank you again for your assistance and cooperation, Miss Holmes." Then, as if as an afterthought, said "You, as well, Doctor."

"You're quite welcome," she said. "Good evening."

Irene shut the door behind them and waited, leaning against the wood, counting the seventeen steps as they descended the

63

stairs. She then turned to Joe, a sly grin on her face.

Joe chuckled and sunk into the chair again. "I knew you agreed to back off too easily. Poor Mr. Cullens has no idea who he's dealing with."

"We're visiting Eddy tomorrow morning," Irene declared. "And we're pulling every single file we need to inspect every inch of this case."

Chapter IV

A Hike Through the Bramble

Irene and Joe frequented Scotland Yard so often that a handful of constables and detective inspectors nodded a hello or gave them a wave as they entered the building. Even though it was later in the morning, men still wandered by with their cups of tea.

Eddy Lestrade happened to be passing through the front lobby when he spotted them. With a mug and a small muffin in his hands, the DI grinned at them as he approached.

"I was thinking of ringing you two tonight," Lestrade said, then his grin dropped. "But you couldn't have known that, so you are not here to discuss what I wanted to chat about…"

Irene brushed some crumbs from his jacket. "That was expert deducing, Inspector."

"Hm," Eddy eyed her suspiciously, but his lips held a hint of amusement. "I suppose I have a moment or two to talk right now. Follow me to my office."

"Office?" Irene wrinkled her nose. "Since when do you have an office?"

"Since I was promoted." He threw a smile over his shoulder and led them toward the rooms at the back. "And you told me you weren't taking any more cases before Christmas."

Joe struggled to keep up as he moved his lanky body through the busy precinct. Meanwhile, Irene, nimble as ever, followed easily, twisting and turning as she pulled her gloves from her hands.

Joe was as tall as the detective inspector but broader, especially in his winter jacket, and didn't even attempt to remove his gloves until he was clear of desks and mail carts.

They reached the office – small and straightforward, housing two desks and a row of filing cabinets.

"I haven't had time to set up any photos," Lestrade admitted, shutting the door with his foot. "But that will come soon enough. I've only just been in here a week."

"You share the room?" Joe glanced curiously at the second desk, but Irene – ever so bold – circled it, studying the papers and personal box of trinkets. She then threw her head back in a roar of laughter, eliciting a sigh from the officer.

"I share with Inspector Gregory. Apparently, we work quite well together."

Irene got her laughter under control. "I will not lie, you two do make a good team."

He shot her a glare as he sat behind his desk while motioning to the two seats on the other side.

"I was going to ring to see what your Christmas plans were. If you had none, then I was going to invite both of you to my father's house for dinner."

Joe was pleasantly surprised by the invite, but hesitated and glanced at Irene. She'd paled at the question.

After a short moment, she cleared her throat.

"Actually, Eddy. I was going to invite *you* to Christmas dinner at Baker Street."

Lestrade leaned back in his chair, and Joe stared at his partner, completely blindsided by her invitation. He thought she'd given up any large Christmas plans as she'd been silent since putting the tree up. He knew that Miss Hudson would cook them up something nice, but with Lestrade being an official guest, they would eat a larger meal with dessert. It would feel like a typical holiday, but one with new friends and family.

A small surge of excitement ran through him, solidifying his choice to stay in London for the season instead of trekking back up north.

Lestrade finally spoke, still a bit taken aback by the invitation. "I would love to, of course. But I do have my own dinner with my family to attend. Nevertheless, surely I can sneak out early to join you for dessert, at least. Are you sure you are ready to host Christmas? I wouldn't want to push you into anything."

Irene waved the detective off, but her actions were stiff. Joe saw the nerves forming in her clenched jaw and jerky movements. "We already have a tree, so what's dinner as well?"

She then looked at him with the panic in her slightly widened eyes.

"Please come for dessert or dinner if you are able," he said to Lestrade, smiling warmly at his friend. Irene visibly relaxed at his offered support.

"Shall I bring anything?"

"I have absolutely no idea how hosting a dinner works," Irene admitted. "So, we will let you know. But I do know that we will have a Christmas goose."

At the same moment, the door behind them swung open and Thom Gregory strode into the room.

"Did I hear something about a Christmas goose?"

"We are having a goose for Christmas dinner," Irene explained.

The newcomer nodded in approval. His new, sharp suit was tailored, the seams of his trousers crisp. His appearance made Joe glance at his own attire and notice that he'd somehow managed two separate, yet equally uneven creases in his legs.

Gregory headed to his desk, nodding at Irene's choice of fowl. "Goose is quite tasty. Are you having a large dinner?"

"Just a small gathering. I assume you are having quite the party, given your list of friends and family?"

Joe and Lestrade watched on with fascination. Irene and Gregory got along better and better these days, though they still teased each other endlessly. However, this conversation felt like it required more privacy than it was given because, in response, the other DI shook his head, chuckling darkly.

"I actually don't see my family since I moved to the city after the war. But finding someone to keep me company shouldn't be too hard."

He winked at Irene before shuffling some folders on his

69

desk.

Joe felt empathetic toward Gregory, but he knew that if he started inviting more and more people to dinner, they'd need multiple geese and more food than Miss Hudson was prepared to make.

In the meantime, Irene was staring at Gregory, chewing her lip, deep in thought. Before Joe could dwell too much on that implication, she spoke:

"You are more than welcome to ring in the new year with us." Her words came quickly, as if trying to get them out before she changed her mind.

Gregory raised an eyebrow and smiled. "You'd really want me there?"

"Yes. Baker Street would be a grand place to celebrate the new year."

The man scooped up a file and happily pointed at her, seeming pleasantly surprised. "I will be there."

When he sauntered out of the room, Irene faced both her remaining friends.

"Since when are we having a New Year's gathering?" Joe asked.

She gestured wildly to Gregory's empty desk. "I couldn't

exactly leave him staring at me like a lost puppy."

Lestrade chuckled. "That would be perfectly in character for you, though."

Irene folded her arms across her chest and huffed. "Well, maybe I'm feeling generous because it's Christmas."

"Or guilty, because you consider Gregory a friend?"

Joe hid his smile as Irene scowled at both of them. "Let's get back to why we are here, shall we? Eddy, we need two files."

The detective held up his hands in an attempt to slow her down. "You can't just demand files. I need a reason to pull them from the cabinets."

"Is the British government enough of a reason?"

*   *   *   *   *

Roughly ten minutes after he left to find the files, Lestrade walked in with a few folders in his hand. Irene went to grab for them, but he pulled them out of her reach.

"I can't let you take these. Not this time. You may look them over in the meeting room down the hall."

Irene shook her head. "That simply won't do."

"It has to."

While Joe would've preferred settling at Baker Street with a cup of tea, he understood Lestrade's concern. The last time they'd taken files with them, they had returned them in a less than desirable condition.

Irene, however, disagreed. She fished a business card from her purse and set it on the DI's desk. "This is Mr. Cullens' card. He will vouch for us."

Eddy picked up the card, sighing. "You cannot simply take files because someone from the government said so."

"Then what is the point of the government if not to supersede the rules of the common detective inspector?"

"You certainly have a way with words, Irene."

It was then that Joe saw a plan forming behind the man's eyes. Lestrade leaned forward, matching Irene's gaze in a challenge.

"I'll make you a deal. I'll let you take these files if you call Marla."

Irene recoiled in confusion. "Your sister?"

He nodded and jotted down Marla's number on a scrap piece of paper.

"This is her new number now that she's settled into a flat with her fiancé. She was asking about you. Now that you are having your own dinner at Baker Street, she won't see you at

Christmas."

"Marla has a fiancé? When did that occur?"

"Don't remind me. He seems like a good chap, but she's still my younger sister, and she's growing up too quickly. Call her, Irene. She'd love to chat."

Irene frowned, but took the paper reluctantly. Before she could pull her hand away, Lestrade clamped his fingers around hers.

"It will be good for you. You must get simply fed up with Joe and me sometimes. Marla's company would do you some good."

Joe felt a soft smile come across his face. He and Eddy had spoken about encouraging their mutual friend to reach out to others. They'd even tried so over the past few weeks with no luck, but perhaps the holidays were a perfect excuse. The two men shared a quick look of hope.

"I suppose one phone call wouldn't hurt," Irene mumbled, tucking the paper into her purse.

"Atta girl," Lestrade gave her a reassuring smile, but she avoided his gaze.

"We should really be going." She stood, done with the conversation.

Joe knew that, with their task complete, they risked getting into personal conversation and small chit-chat territory, and Irene didn't appear to have time for any of that – today was all business. Even her offer of the New Year's party to Gregory was tactful.

They said their goodbyes and Lestrade walked them to the front of the building.

"Oh!" he exclaimed before they left. "Do you still have the camera I lent you?"

Joe opened his mouth to confirm that they did, in fact, still have the camera, and they'd used it just yesterday, but Irene spoke over top of him.

"I'd have to check," she said quickly. "But I'm certain I returned it at some point."

The detective inspector frowned. "Hm, I will look again, but I didn't see it there."

"Thank you for the files," Irene added, shooting a warning glance at her partner. "We will return them as soon as we've done our research."

Joe kept his mouth shut as instructed, shaking his head in amused disbelief as he followed Irene out of the building.

The dining room table at 221B was full of papers from the various folders that Joe and Irene had collected at Scotland Yard. She looked over the assassination attempt on Mr. Timothy Aston while Joe perused the folder pertaining to the taxicab accident.

"This is a sad tale," he said, frowning at the notes on the car crash. "A taxicab, driven by a man named George Henley, went through a red light and hit Ryan Inglis. The driver cooperated with the constables – appeared very apologetic – then was taken into custody. That night, he apparently became so distraught with grief and guilt that he begged the constables to release him. When they refused, the man hanged himself."

Irene scooted over beside him, half a cup of tea in her hand, and quickly scanned the documents. "That is certainly interesting. We'll have to visit the cab company and find out a little more about him. I'm curious as to what kind of person he was and if he had a history of accidents. Now, come here and look at what I've got. It's something just as interesting."

Rather than move his chair, Joe simply stood behind her, leaning down over her shoulder with one hand on the table.

Irene paraphrased the long paragraphs of case notes from the file.

"Mr. Aston claims he was riding in the fields with his hunting dogs. He heard the shot; it spooked the horse, which reared, causing him to fall. The dogs went into a frenzy and took off into the woods, and Mr. Aston followed. He claims he found nothing as the forest is very overgrown and dense."

Joe skimmed the notes and found the conclusion from Scotland Yard. "They seem to corroborate his statement. Their constables couldn't get through to the river because the bramble and roots were so bad, one man even twisted his ankle."

Irene was silent for a moment. She grasped the teacup close to her lips, staring off into the flat. Joe knew that look and sighed, dragging his feet back to his own chair.

"You want to climb through that bramble, don't you?"

"What if they missed something? Which, knowing Scotland Yard, they most certainly did."

"Irene," Joe warned, though he knew there was no talking her out of it. "This took place five months ago. Whatever may have been there is probably lost by now."

"I would still like to look," she said, compiling the papers back into their folders.

"We can definitely look, but don't hold your breath."

*　　*　　*　　*　　*

Joe tugged his coat tighter around his neck as he and Irene made their way across the backfield of the Aston estate. They approached the dark forest on either side of the river flowing through the property. Joe shook his head at the sight. Even from here, he could tell the forest floor was overgrown with roots, weeds, and thick bramble.

Irene, shoulders set in determination, slipped into the woods, wiggling around the trees with expert precision.

He followed as best he could, letting out a grunt here and there. More than once, he bumped his head on a low branch or caught a sleeve on prickly thorns. At one point, he stretched his leg over a large root and felt a strong pull on his inner thigh. Tomorrow, his body would be sore, scratched, and stiff. While he didn't mind the physical work, Joe hoped that this expedition was worth the time and struggle that he and Irene endured right now.

They'd spent the better part of thirty minutes clamouring through the forest when he heard the faint sound of rushing water. They came upon a clearing with just enough room for them to stand shoulder to shoulder.

The river was barely audible beyond a thick tangle of roots and bushes, preventing access to the edge of the shallow ravine.

Some small animal scurried away and a large bird cawed in the distance. The woods were eerie and conjured up images of the fantasy lands Joe read about in his novels.

Despite the dirt on her hands, Irene pressed her finger to her lips. Joe felt useless beside her, so he attempted to search for... something. Broken branches? Footprints? It had been so long since a potential shooter had been here that all trace would surely be lost. To him, anyway.

His partner crouched and poked around, pausing every now and then to examine a twig or leaf at closer inspection. Her entire face contorted into a scowl every time she came up empty-handed.

A large root formed a barrier between the clearing and the edge of the river. Irene folded herself in half, attempting to squeeze through it.

Joe groaned and reached out to grab her, but she was too quick.

"Irene! Do be careful, please. The river is just on the other side."

"I'm fine, Joe," she called, then disappeared into the tangle of vines and leaves.

He hurried forward, quickly picking his own way through. A branch tore his jacket sleeve and he stumbled, a rough branch skinning his palm. Through a thinning bush, the edge of the river was visible. The water had dropped at least ten feet, but Joe still heard it trickle through.

Irene's blue coat flashed through the bushes. He heard her let out a startled cry, and then she was gone.

"Irene!" Joe hurried through the thicket, cringing as a loud splash came from below. He emerged at the small ravine, the river at least forty feet across. The edge on the opposite side was rough and unstable. Roots clawed their way out of the ground and walls like some enraged monster breaking free from prison.

Joe approached the edge, looking down. His breath steamed the cold air. He only saw half of the river rushing by, but his friend was nowhere in sight.

"Irene!" His heart was in his throat. A fall from that height was survivable, but if Irene landed the wrong way, she'd be seriously hurt.

Joe shimmied along the edge, trying to find a way down. He

heard sloshing, like footsteps, and hoped that the sound was his partner walking through the water.

He crouched, ready to swing down blindly, when he heard a voice, excited and elated, from below.

"Joe!" Irene called. "Come quick. I've found our shooter!"

Chapter V

A Curious Piece to the Puzzle

Irene stared at the body still caught in the roots and weeds. The man's arms were splayed and twisted in branches sticking out from the side of the ravine. One leg was hidden under mud, the other hung limp, and the water was attempting to drag the man's foot downstream. Mould and fungi grew on the dark, damp clothes; the fabric clung to the bloated green-hued skin.

Irene inched closer, yanking her shoes from the mud with each step. A large cut split the man's temple in two – the cause of death. Her heart raced with excitement at the grotesque scene. She couldn't wait to get the body examined and find out his identity.

Branches snapped behind her. Then she heard Joe huffing and puffing. He let out a panicked cry. Irene turned just as he slipped down the wall of dirt and into the shallow water.

He managed to catch himself, landing on his hands and feet like a lanky bear. Irene immediately went to him.

She helped her partner stand, leaving dirty handprints on his clothes. His nose wrinkled as he shook the clumps of mud from his hand, wiping the rest on his jacket.

He looked up at the small cliff they'd both slid down.

"How the hell are we going to get back up?"

"We'll figure that out later," she said, tugging his sleeve. "Come and see this."

They marched back to the body, slipping and bumping into one another. Their shoes squelched in the mud, their breath fogging the air in front of them. When they arrived at the tangled mess, Irene gestured to the poor victim.

Joe let out a gargled, disgusted cry and recoiled, slipping on the wet bank and nearly falling.

"This body looks worse than the woman we found in the attic a few months ago. Who is that?"

"Our shooter," Irene replied simply. "He must've tripped while running from the dogs and stumbled into the river, cracking his head in the process. You saw all those rocks back there."

"I did," Joe said, still inching away from the body.

Irene looked further downstream for some other clue as to what happened to this man. A long, dark brown and silver object caught her attention about twenty feet away. Moving downstream, she eventually came upon the item, a grin spreading across her face.

A British army sniper rifle stuck into the side of the bank, half covered in mud. Gnarled branches curled around the barrel, securing it to the wall.

Irene gripped the gun and pulled. It shifted, but the vines had wrapped so tightly around it that she'd need some pruning scissors to cut them.

Joe came up behind her, his voice chattering from the cold. "What do we do now?"

She turned to him and frowned in pity. His poor nose was red, the colour spreading to his cheeks. The damp ends of his sleeves and the hem of his pants were stiffening due to the cold.

"We cannot move that body on our own. Nor do we have the tools to free that rifle. So, we climb back up and telephone Scotland Yard."

She scoured the wall of dirt and roots towering above them for any sort of way to get to the top.

Joe joined her, shivering as he conducted his own survey.

83

"If you can boost me up to that root." Irene pointed to a knot of trees about halfway up the embankment. "I can pull myself up, then assist you."

He hooked his fingers together to make a step, then crouched. She steadied herself using his shoulders and stepped into his gloved hands, mud squishing over his wrists. Hoisted up, she grabbed for the root but missed entirely and collapsed backwards. Both of them crashed into the shallow water with a shriek and loud splash.

Irene tensed as the cold water rushed through her clothes, freezing her skin. Joe let out a string of cuss words that she'd never heard him speak before. In a frenzy of splashing water, they both scrambled to their feet, pausing for a moment to catch their breaths, then tried again.

This time, Irene grasped the root and kicked her feet, trying to gain traction on the mud. She got a foothold and launched herself higher, grabbing another root. By the time she made it to the top, her arms burned. Laying on her stomach, she extended her hand to Joe. He grasped the root with ease and was up in less time than she was. Hand in his, she dragged him up beside her.

For a moment, they laid side by side in the bramble and

mud, shoulders touching, chests heaving.

Then he sat up, expression thoroughly disgusted. "I truly hated that. Let's hope Scotland Yard has better luck."

*　　*　　*　　*　　*

The two investigators huddled together and watched four constables and three rescue workers hack their way through the bramble to get to the river. A caravan sat outside of the forest, full of excavating equipment, ready to pull the body and rifle up when the workers reached it.

Eddy had been both shocked and exasperated at Irene's phone call but promised to come out right away. He now stood next to them, watching his men work through the thicket.

Irene shivered and glanced at Joe. Eddy had suggested they both stay indoors, but she wanted to be there every step of the way to make sure Scotland Yard missed nothing.

Over an hour later, they brought the body out on a stretcher. Away from the branches, the victim looked even more bloated, the skin darkened in odd places as it was jostled from its original position.

Eddy cussed and turned to her. "I need to prepare myself

better for when you call me to retrieve a body. You have a knack for finding the most grotesque ones."

Irene tried to chuckle, but it came out stuttered.

Her detective friend scowled. "Go home. We've retrieved everything properly. Take some linen from the caravan so you don't dirty your car and return to Baker Street."

She nodded in agreement. "I want the autopsy as soon as possible, Eddy. Bribe the coroner if you must."

He bunched his shoulders against the cold. "I am quite curious as well, as we had closed this case. I didn't tend to it personally, but I remember it passing by my desk. I will do my best to get results."

"Thank you." Then, she turned to her partner who looked like a frozen statue, nose and cheeks completely red, big shivers shaking his body. "Oh, dear. Come on, let's get home quickly. Take care, Eddy."

The inspector gave them a wave as they headed toward the Vauxhall parked in the laneway. Irene stopped off at the caravan to grab two sheets, then quickly caught up to Joe. She was as cold as he looked, but this case's excitement stirred some heat inside. She was eager to find out just who this shooter was and hopefully figure out why he took aim at Mr. Aston.

The warmth of 221B felt like Heaven itself had opened up.

Irene's goal was to attempt to clean up before Miss Hudson spotted them, but as their luck would have it, she exited her first floor flat and spotted the pair before they'd even reached the stairs to their own flat.

The woman gasped, then made sputtering noises as her eyes swept over them.

"We're so sorry, Miss Hudson," Joe said, his voice still hoarse from the cold.

The housekeeper drew closer, shaking her head. "Did you both fall into a lake? Or is the weather that terrible out? Wait, is that mud? What on earth happened?"

Irene waved her off, suddenly too tired and cold. The dampness was causing her clothes to stick to her skin, suffocating her. "We fell into a river attempting to locate a body. We'd really like to wash up now."

"And you most certainly will," Miss Hudson took immediate charge of them, shuffling them toward the stairs, tracking mud. "Joe, you wait right there, love. Irene, you take off those shoes and head directly into my flat."

When they both looked at her for further explanation, she sighed, exasperated at their questioning.

"I'm scrubbing your hair clean, myself, Missy. And Joe here is going to wait until we're inside my flat, and he's going to strip down and leave his clothes right here. Then he will take the upstairs lavatory. Go on now."

Irene's shoulders started to ache and she didn't feel like arguing. She moved slowly down the hall, the landlady right on her heels, stealing one last glance at Joe to make sure he hadn't fallen over. He'd taken the cold and water much worse than she had.

Miss Hudson must've taken the glance as something indecent because she swatted her shoulder.

"Never you mind looking at him."

"I wasn't..." But the strength left her completely and Irene let the old woman lead her into the flat.

*   *   *   *   *

Irene sat back against the bathtub's outer edge, tugging her robe tighter. Her body had come clean in the warm water, but she was so chilled that it felt as if she'd never be warm again. Now, she sat on a small stool, staring up at Miss Hudson's ceiling, as the landlady added some more shampoo to her hair, scrubbing deep with her fingernails.

Miss Hudson grabbed a jug of water and poured it over her head, doing the fourth rinse back into the tub. Startled at the temperature, Irene stubbed her toe on the sink.

"Ouch! I don't remember this room being so small."

"The last time I washed your hair like this, you were half the size."

"Was it that long ago?"

"Yes."

Before, Irene had been more than hesitant to recall those memories. Now, she allowed herself a tiny crack in the door of her mind. She realized it *had* been a long while. As a child, there was either no time or it was of no priority to wash her hair as often as it should've been, yet she was desperate to keep it long. Miss Hudson would plunk her down on this very stool she sat upon now and scrub until every speck of dirt was out, then plait the locks before sending the little girl on her way.

Twenty years later, Irene was slightly taller and broader, but her head tugged just the same as Miss Hudson combed through the damp strands. She felt like a child again. Soon, she'd be ready to run upstairs with fresh plaits and curl up by the fire to listen to Uncle John read his latest story about her father.

"I want to do Christmas dinner at Baker Street," Irene said before her mind could dwell on her memories any longer. "The three of us, and possibly Eddy. And I would like a goose."

Miss Hudson paused and leaned over her, eclipsing the lamp hanging over the tub. She was silent for a moment, then her wrinkled cheeks spread in a broad grin.

"Oh, Irene! I would be delighted to make dinner. Your father was always partial to a goose."

The woman squeezed her hair to get out the water, then tapped her shoulder. Irene got up, stretching her shoulders, her muscles stiff from the day.

"Thank you. In advance."

Miss Hudson tut-tutted. "You know it's no trouble. I am proud of you, love. Christmas dinner is a big step. You've done quite well."

Irene's ears grew warm as she played with the tie on her robe. She spun on the stool and faced the wall as Miss Hudson rubbed her hair with a towel. Her head bobbed up and down as the older woman tugged and dried the strands.

"I am going to pay your father a visit over the holidays," Miss Hudson told her, words crisp and clear as if she'd practised the sentence in her head a few times before speaking. "You are more than welcome to come."

At first, the words didn't register in Irene's mind. She kept staring at the wall as Miss Hudson started on the plait. The old woman knew better than to ask as the answer was always the same.

"You know I don't want to," Irene said dismissively, tightening the belt anxiously around her waist.

"I thought I'd offer. This year has been quite different for you, and I thought you might change your mind."

A thousand excuses came up, but Irene didn't say any of them. Both knew that any reason she'd give for not seeing her father was simply that – an excuse.

However, she had to admit to herself that her curiosity about her father's health grew more and more with each passing week. It hurt her heart every time she thought of him. Miss Hudson was correct in one thing: Irene had taken a step forward by deciding to celebrate Christmas at Baker Street. Yet could she handle any news on her father?

"How..." She trailed off, took a breath, then tried again.

"How is..."

She couldn't bring herself to ask. A lump formed in her throat, tears pricking her eyes. She was not as brave as she'd thought herself to be.

"He is the same." The landlady answered anyway, halfway done with the plait. "He still reads up a storm. That seems to be the only place where his mind is itself. Music also keeps him grounded as he loves listening to the phonograph. Winters are the hardest, though."

Irene blinked, two tears rolled down her cheek.

"I don't know if I can do it, Miss Hudson. I don't know if I could visit him. I don't know if I could handle seeing him how he is now, simply a shell of his former self. I'd rather have the last image of him to be who he was ten years ago. Clever, strong, happy..."

Another tear rolled down her cheek and Irene sniffled.

The old woman secured the plait and put her hands on Irene's shoulders, gently turning her on the stool and wiping her tears away.

"You will still have those images of him. But – and I say this with all the love and experience in my heart – don't wait too long to see him one last time. I know you, Irene. You'll be mad at yourself for the rest of your life if you miss an opportunity to say goodbye."

Irene's bottom lip trembled, but she managed a nod.

"Life gets tough, and change is hard. Even if it is for the better. But you're tough, Irene Holmes." Miss Hudson patted her head then pulled her in for a hug. "Now, you're still freezing. Get on upstairs and make sure Joe is thawed out. I'll warm some stew and be up shortly."

Irene stood and tugged her robe tight, then left the first floor flat. All the way up the seventeen steps to her own, she breathed deep, ridding her throat of the painful lump. Pausing at the small mirror just outside the door, she made sure her eyes weren't red.

Before entering, she rolled her shoulders and took a few quick breaths in an attempt to pull the mask back on that she knew she wore occasionally. She didn't need Joe asking if she 'was okay' because she didn't want to even think about anything more tonight. She was ready for stew and a good night's sleep.

She flung the door open in her usual reckless manner and strode into the sitting room.

Sarah James sat on the couch across from Joe, turning to smiled at Irene. Her dark blue eyes then got a good look at her robe and wet plaited hair, and she looked momentarily surprised and concerned.

"Hello, Sarah." Irene flashed her a polite smile and wandered to her desk, noting Joe's damp hair, tousled and uncombed, himself in lounging clothes and a robe.

The woman stumbled over her words. "Sorry, was I interrupting something?"

"Not at all. We just took a tumble down a hill and needed to wash off."

Irene poked at the daily mail on her desk while Joe stammered out more of an explanation from his chair.

"We have separate lavatories."

"You guys sound like you have quite the adventures." Sarah laughed, but Irene caught the unsure tone. "I'm not going to stay long. I just thought I would pop by and see you."

Irene watched the woman bat her eyelashes at Joe. Something told her that she should give them privacy, but she really didn't want to be in her bedroom alone, especially after how her conversation with Miss Hudson ended.

The other woman eyed Irene. "Sorry, but am I in your seat? I can sit—"

"No," she snapped as Sarah pointed to the chair closest to the fireplace. "Those pillows stay right there."

94

"Oh! Are they there for a case? Are you trying to work something out?"

"They are not for a case. They just need to stay there."

"Sorry." Sarah sounded confused but turned her attention back to Joe. "Shall we get breakfast tomorrow morning?"

"Oh, that would be lovely," he said, leaning forward.

Irene walked over to the kitchenette and rummaged through the cupboards for some biscuits or something to fidget with.

Sarah and Joe continued their giggly, flirty conversation, which made her sigh. It was as if they'd just met even after a whole month. She more than welcomed a content Joe, but a giggly, flirty one made her feel awkward.

"We are busy tomorrow morning, I'm afraid," she suddenly interjected and popped a hard biscuit in her mouth.

"We are?" Joe asked, turning his curious gaze to her.

"We're reviewing the results of the autopsy. Though I joked about bribing the coroner, Eddy will surely do that as he is just as interested in this case now that it involves Scotland Yard."

"Ah." He looked at the ground, clearly disappointed.

Irene felt a wee bit guilty and thought about offering to go to Scotland Yard on her own tomorrow, but Sarah spoke before she could get her thought out.

95

"That's fine," she told her sweetheart. "What about dinner?"

For whatever reason, Irene found her ever-present compliance with their interfering plans mildly annoying, but she simply crunched her biscuit.

"I could do dinner," Joe replied.

"Oh, wonderful!" The woman giggled and stood. "I'd best get going then."

"I shall drive you home."

Sarah's eyes were sparkling. "Lovely."

"Don't be long," Irene said a little sharper than she meant to. "Miss Hudson is warming stew."

Joe looked rather annoyed, but nodded.

When he and Sarah headed to the door, the woman stopped and tugged at her chestnut hair before addressing them both.

"There is a get-together at the library on Friday. A small group of writers and some of my friends. Both of you are more than welcome to come. There will be tea and discussion. I'm sure you both have such interesting stories to tell – Irene especially. I know my friends would simply die to hear some of your tales."

Joe answered before Irene could give him any kind of signal.

"I will definitely be there. It sounds rather enjoyable. Irene?"

96

Sarah looked at her with a pleasant smile.

"Sure," Irene replied without thinking it through.

"Wonderful!" Sarah chimed. "Goodnight, Irene."

The couple left the flat, laughing and making eyes at one another. Irene shut the door behind them. She opened and closed her mouth a few times, the stale biscuit she still chewed drying out her mouth.

A gathering at the library sounded both horrid and intriguing. She loved discussions of various subjects but tended to over-explain most things as she almost always knew a great deal more than whoever she was speaking to. But if appearing at the gathering would make Joe happy, she'd do it.

Since he began seeing Sarah seriously, Irene had made her best effort to include the happy woman in her life as someone important to Joe. Sarah wasn't annoying – as some people could be – and she did tolerate Irene and all her quirks. On the other hand, Joe had changed the way he interacted with her, his new relationship tying up many of his evenings, leaving Irene all by herself in the flat.

But he seemed much happier – that's what mattered, wasn't it? The obvious answer was *yes*, but as Irene paid more attention to people's feelings, she found that a small bit of resentment crept in every now and then. Occasionally, she wished she could feel as happy as others seemed to feel.

Cases made her happy. Mystery and intrigue made her mind work, gave her a thrill. But it was the time between investigations, the having to deal with real life part, where she felt lost. And as the days went on, it was as if she was losing her way even more.

Irene puffed, accidentally spraying biscuit crumbs onto the floor. Feelings were useless and weighed her down, and she hated how strongly she felt them.

Marching to the sink in the kitchenette, she turned the tap on and stuck her head under the water for a rather large gulp to wash the rest of the biscuit down. Wiping her face with her sleeve, she plunked down at the dining table and pouted as she waited for her stew.

Chapter VI

Extending a New Year's Invitation

Joe stared out the window, watching the traffic, as Irene drove them both to Scotland Yard the following morning. She seemed distracted, which occasionally was her normal, especially if deep in thought about a case. Today, however, she appeared to be right on the edge of biting someone's hand off if they moved too quickly around her.

"I'm glad we're having Christmas dinner together," Joe ventured. "And it was quite lovely of you to invite Lestrade, despite him only able to arrive after the meal. I haven't spoken to Sarah about it yet, but hopefully, she can make it even if just for afterwards as well."

"Sarah?" Irene sounded completely perplexed for a moment.

Joe sighed. He thought he might get some push back regarding his girlfriend coming to dinner, but he figured it was worth a try. Before he could speak again or give his reasoning, Irene carried on with her sentence.

"I hadn't realized you wanted to invite her to our dinner."

She sounded as if trying to keep the contempt from her voice, and Joe had to at least appreciate the attempt. He still felt a bit defensive of his relationship, which may have been the cause for his next words coming out a little quick.

"It's my Christmas dinner too."

Irene's hand tightened on the steering wheel.

He bristled at the potential argument.

"Of course, it's your dinner as well," she replied stiffly. "I just thought we were inviting people we considered family, and friends we were reserving for New Year's."

"I don't believe we'd discussed that."

"I thought it was rather obvious."

He didn't want to argue this morning, especially about Christmas or Sarah, both of which were touchy subjects. He did, however, feel some sort of need to defend himself.

"It wasn't obvious," he sighed, tugging at his leather gloves. "But it's fine. A small Christmas dinner will be nice. I will invite her to our New Year's gathering instead."

Irene pulled into a spot against the curb in front of Scotland

Yard.

"Do whatever you like, Joe."

With that, the conversation was done.

Usually, their arguments were based around small misunderstandings and quickly resolved, but this one felt different. Like it was touching upon issues that were not easily talked over a cup of tea.

Joe's ribs squeezed his lungs at the start of a small panic-induced episode that he hadn't had in months.

Irene shut the automobile off and exited without another word. He took as calm a breath as he could, then stepped out into the damp December air, attempting to clear his lungs.

*   *   *   *   *

Neither one of them spoke as they waited in Lestrade's office, which again, wasn't abnormal, but Joe hated the tension circling them. Perhaps he was the only one because Irene seemed as normal as ever, eager to investigate the autopsy file.

As if on cue, Lestrade entered the office. He'd barely made it through the door when Irene snatched the papers from his hand. He scowled as sat at his desk, crossing his arms.

Ignoring him, Irene slid close to Joe and opened the file for both of them to read. Whatever awkwardness had been there seemed to dissipate and Joe was eternally grateful.

"You definitely manage to find doozies, don't you?" Lestrade observed, lighting a cigarette. "I'm leading the investigation on this man, but any help from you is more than welcome this time."

Irene smirked at him. "Working with the government does have its advantages for private investigators like us."

Joe was about to speak aloud, but she continued, paraphrasing the report.

"Two fingers missing from a past incident well before his death. A broken ankle, a split in his temple, and a snapped neck, possibly from being chased by the dogs and falling into the ravine. He also has a tattoo."

She pulled a photo from behind the report. The lettering on the tattoo was shaky and crude, as if done with primitive equipment or an unsteady hand:

MOUNTAIN II

Joe looked closer, noticing scarred scratches around the words, and he couldn't for the life of him figure out what those would be.

Irene took out other photos of the victim's clothes and

spread them on the desk. The military jacket was easily identifiable, even spotted with mould and water, but cleaned up enough to show the grey-green colour. All the patches had been ripped off, giving no clue as to which faction of the man had served. The tattoo was their only clue.

"I am sorely lacking in my knowledge of military tattoos and will have to rectify that as soon as I am able. Joe, do you know this?"

He shook his head. "I do not, unfortunately. But, with the number of men who served in this building, surely someone knows."

Just then Thom Gregory walked in with a cup of coffee. All three heads turned to him, causing the man to freeze, his eyes wide.

"Shall I run away before you pounce on me?"

"Please don't," Irene retorted. "Come here and look at this. We require your knowledge."

"You've never asked for my assistance on a case. And certainly not my knowledge."

"Sure we have. We did on our last case."

"I assisted Joe in proper tea attire." Gregory set his coffee on his desk and walked over to them, then studied the photo of the tattoo.

"Mountain? Those were the Scots." He leaned closer, brow furrowed in thought. "It looks like there was an attempt to remove it." He pointed at the outer parts of the word, where the scratches were. "I knew a sailor whose tattoos used to give him nightmares so bad he carved his skin off. These look like similar, though a failed attempt, for sure."

Irene glanced at Joe, who simply shook his head in disbelief. Between the ripped patches and the tattoo removal attempt, it was clear that whoever this man was, he wanted to disassociate himself from the British army since returning from war.

She stood and paced around the room, a finger to her lips.

Lestrade poked at the photo of the tattoo. "Finding out exactly who this man is will prove difficult."

Irene paused her pacing to look at the inspectors. "Could we find him, though?"

Gregory nodded. "Eventually. But it could take all day while we exhaust our resources."

"Excellent. Joe and I have a taxicab company to visit. If you both could look into the soldier and find us someone else in his regiment who lives in or around London, that will make all the difference. We shall meet back here for afternoon tea."

Gregory waved his hand at her in a panic. "Hold on, Irene. Lestrade has already claimed this case, and I have my own work to do."

She looked between the two inspectors. "Then you both shall lay claim to it. As Eddy will tell you, this takes priority – it pertains to a bigger investigation concerning the government. Thank you, gentlemen. See you this afternoon."

With those words, she pivoted and left the room.

Lestrade called after her, "Wait! You still haven't fully explained *how* this connects to the government!"

Joe paused, ready to tell them about Mr. Cullens, but Irene popped back into the room.

"Come, Joe! We've got a drive across the city to make."

* * * * *

The two sat in the small office across from a sweaty, ageing man named Richard, who looked like he aged a year in a day due to stress. He had papers scattered on every surface and two telephones on his desk.

"Everyone is going everywhere these days," he said, wiping sweat off his brow with a handkerchief. "I can't grow quick

105

enough."

"That is good, then?" Joe offered.

He blew out a breath. "It is, yes. Sorry. You wanted to ask me questions?"

Irene nodded. "We were looking for more information on the accident that occurred in March involving George Henley."

"I'm proud to say that we don't have many accidents like that one. With winter coming up, though, I hope that ice stays away. Lord knows we don't need—"

"How long had George been working for you at the time of the crash?" Irene interjected.

"Not long. A month or so, maybe less. Quiet guy. Heard he hanged himself after he was arrested. Shame, really."

"Can you tell us anything more about him?"

"Unfortunately, I can't. He never spoke much. Just did his job and clocked out."

"Anything would help," Joe added. "Where he was from, if he had any family, or if he spoke with any sort of accent."

The man shrugged. "Sounded a bit northern, but otherwise didn't mention family or even friends. Didn't even mention where he'd served. Just wanted a job as quick as possible."

Irene stared at Richard so long that he began to squirm.

Finally, she stood.

"Thank you. Good afternoon."

Joe scrambled to keep up with her speed.

They hurried through the row of waiting cabs and out into the street, heading to their automobile.

As soon as they were in the car, Irene clapped her hands together.

"Things are coming together, Joe."

"Are they? Because this seems to confuse me even more. Perhaps this George fellow simply wasn't suited to drive taxi cabs."

"Or," she began, and he caught the wolfish grin on her face. "He took the job for one specific purpose. When that purpose was fulfilled, he was directed to end his own life. Or was feared enough by his instructor that he chose the fate himself."

Joe's eyes widened. Meanwhile, Irene drove along the streets of London, so sure of her dark theory that the smile stayed on her face.

Unease stirred in his stomach.

"What are you saying?" he asked, furrowing his brows. "The only reason he went to work at the taxicab company was to target Ryan Inglis?"

His partner shrugged. "Perhaps. If that is the case, then this mystery grows even larger."

*   *   *   *   *

The search for the dead soldier's name took Lestrade and Gregory all afternoon. The latter of the officers kept reminding Joe and Irene that he had to trade in at least two favours to gather the information, so they had better have decent alcohol at the New Year's party to make up for it.

The mystery man's name was Frank Charles. He'd served with the 52nd Infantry Division.

Apparently, those members were difficult to track down, but Inspector Gregory had managed to find Kenneth Bradley, who lived up in Camden.

In the early evening, as the sun was setting on London, Joe and Irene sat across from Kenneth in his simple sitting room, sipping on tea, ready to hear the soldier's story.

When they'd told the man that they'd recovered Frank Charles' body, he didn't seem surprised. Irene mentioned it was found in an odd place – without revealing too much detail – and still, the former soldier remained stoic. He didn't press them for any other information, merely ran his hands through his short dark hair, nodded solemnly and lit a cigarette.

"Frank was the best shooter in the regiment. And he knew it. He was ruthless. 'A born killer made for war' is what Command said about him. He was in his element out on the battlefield."

"Frank had a tattoo," Irene added quietly. "On his forearm."

A sad smile came over Kenneth's face, and he rolled up his sleeve, revealing his own 'Mountain II' tattoo.

"We all got one once we'd passed basic training because we were damn proud of being there. If I'd known I was going to make it through the war, I would've picked a nicer design."

He gave a soft chuckle, flicking the ashes from his cigarette.

Joe paused his note-taking and remembered the ripped patches and scratched tattoo from Frank's autopsy photos. "Frank was as proud as the rest of you?"

"Yes. He remained proud right up until the week he disappeared."

"Where did he disappear from?" Irene asked.

Kenneth hesitated, and Joe recognized it instantly. This man didn't want to speak about the war, which was truly understandable.

"Mr. Bradley, we know this is difficult, and we don't intend to force you to speak about anything you do not wish to reveal."

He felt Irene shift beside him – impatient, no doubt.

"Though," she added, "any information you can provide us will greatly assist in the case."

Kenneth nodded in understanding and took a long drag on his cigarette in preparation. He sighed, the smoke blowing out his mouth, then he spoke: "We were captured and taken to a camp, and all of us worried that Frank would be the first to die, whether by sheer mental breakdown or by one of the guards. From the moment we were taken to the camp, Frank was belligerent and didn't obey our captors. He went days without food, was beaten.

"Hardest thing I ever did was survive that camp, and I was lucky to come out intact and with my sanity. Most of us just kept our heads down and got through one day at a time. Frank had the worst time of it, though. The days started to break him. They cut off his fingers to force his co-operation."

The man stared down at his cigarette. Joe recognized the haunting look behind his eyes; he had just barely overcome his own nightmares and panic-induced episodes. He'd been fortunate enough to only be held by a small group of German soldiers, and he simply couldn't imagine what life was like in the POW camps.

Irene gave the veteran a minute to bring himself out of his memories, which made Joe felt a wee bit proud. A few months ago, she would've barrelled through the conversation.

After a few moments, she spoke: "Did something significant happen in the camp that altered his personality in some way?"

Kenneth frowned. "One day, the guards grabbed him and dragged him away. He was gone for hours. He looked like he'd seen a ghost when he returned. He was instantly distrustful of all of us, even though we'd served with him for years. He didn't speak much for the next two days, then they took him again. This time, when he returned, he had a fit. He ripped off all the patches on his uniform and tried to scratch his tattoo off."

A tremor went through his hand as he recalled the memory.

Joe shifted on the couch. He knew they had to question the soldier, but he felt sympathetic. He hadn't even told Sarah much about the war, so he understood the trepidation that the soldier felt as two strangers asked him to remember details about a horrible time of his life.

If Irene had any reservations about continuing the interview, she kept it to herself and asked another question. "Can you think of any more details, no matter how small?"

"There may be something, but it may also be nonsense."

"Nothing is nonsense when dealing with facts. Continue."

"A group of us saw a nice automobile drive to the main house," Kenneth spoke low, clearly not confident with his story. "We thought nothing of it, but it arrived the day Frank was taken away, and it came back the next few days as well. The following week, they took Frank away for one final time – this time for good. I don't know if one has to do with the other, but like you said, you wanted the facts."

Irene nodded.

Joe found the story curious. "Did you ever see who drove this particular automobile?"

"I didn't. Wally, our explosives man, swears he saw a woman driving it, and going in and out of the house. He claims he saw her one day while he was figuring out a way to escape. I don't know how much of that is true because we were hungry and delirious, but he swears it."

Irene leaned forward. Joe could practically feel her vibrating with excitement. "Was this a tall, blonde woman?"

Kenneth thought for a moment. "Possibly. I'm trying to recall what Wally said. I think it was about a blonde. Said it was an angel, either way."

Joe knew they were done with the interview, especially when he saw Irene giving her signature curt nod. Kenneth had supplied them with a possible connection between AB, Frank Charles and the attempted assassination of Timothy Aston.

"Thank you, Kenneth," she said, pulling out their card. "Just in case you need our services, don't hesitate to call. You've provided us with valuable information."

She turned and headed to the front door, the eagerness poorly disguised in her steps.

Kenneth stuttered, now apparently deciding to ask all the questions he'd been storing in his mind. "Is that it? How did Frank die? What—"

"We, unfortunately, cannot reveal any more than that, but you have been accommodating," Joe intervened.

"Have I?" The man appeared dumbfounded. "If you say so."

"You have." Joe shook his hand, desperately attempting to make up for Irene's tactless departure. "We shall ring you once we have more information. Again, thank you for your time, and you will hear from us with any news. Have a good evening."

Kenneth walked with him to the door and gave a final wave to Irene who was already down on the pavement.

Joe jogged down the stairs, shivering at the cool evening air, as his partner tugged her gloves.

"I knew it, Joe! AB has been more involved in this scheme than Mr. Cullens realised."

"You really think she's behind this?" Joe asked as they approached the Vauxhall.

"Yes," Irene said, pausing before opening the door. "And I don't believe she's done yet."

They climbed in and she started the engine.

While they drove back to Baker Street, a small smile came across Joe's face. This was the Irene he was used to – who bopped up and down with excitement while on a case. Who was sharp-witted and clever. Because her mood had been so off lately, it was a breath of fresh air to see her so eager.

"AB's plan to kill Timothy Aston failed the first time," she said, hands tapping the steering wheel. "So, she will try again. I just don't know how yet."

Joe spoke out loud as ideas came to him. "If they weren't part of the same case, you'd swear AB had a hand in the death of Bernadette's husband as well. But to what end? Would she have known that Bernadette would marry Timothy? Did she plan that too?"

"Remember those thoughts, Joe. We shall write everything

down on our board, but I believe that AB has been running these people's lives for months now."

*   *   *   *   *

They were barely home for twenty minutes before Mr. Cullens and Mr. Digby came calling.

The government officials both seemed a tad disappointed with the pair, but it was Mr. Digby who addressed their frustration once all were sat with a cup of tea in the flat.

"We've received word that you've been investigating into other matters. We need you—"

"By whom?" Irene asked, perched upon the armrest of Joe's chair. She had her arms folded, clearly indignant of the conversation.

"We have sources, Miss Holmes."

Mr. Cullens jumped in, speaking more soothingly than his partner. "Mr. Digby went to pull a file from Scotland Yard, which someone else had already taken. The case had been reopened by a Detective Inspector Lestrade, who we've been told works with you quite often."

"You're correct. I've furthered the investigation and

115

discovered many important facts worth noting."

"Miss Holmes," Mr Digby huffed, "we asked you to do a simple job—"

"I am." Irene cut him off sharply, causing Joe to suck in a breath of worry. "And that job has led me down this particular path, which now includes the death of someone who was indeed in the woods with the intention to shoot Mr. Aston *and* a connection to the very woman we are all here to stop before she does even more damage."

Mr. Cullens lifted his hands as if to soothe two wild animals. "I understand your need to continue with this, Miss Holmes, but our hope was to keep this task simple."

"Simple doesn't always work out. At one point, we thought the war would be simple."

The younger man sighed. Joe could tell he was attempting to keep his frustration with Irene *and* Mr. Digby contained.

"Because Scotland Yard has the file open again, we will instruct them to give us whatever new findings they have, as well as the information you've gathered. You've done a lot, giving us many different paths to go down and options to think about, and I thank you greatly."

"We've got it from here," Mr. Digby cut in.

"Got it from here?" Irene repeated. "I have good reason to believe that AB recruited Frank Charles from a prison camp and has been using him as an assassin for God knows how long. I also believe that she orchestrated the accident that led to the death of Bernadette's husband, Ryan Inglis."

Joe kept silent, attempting to support his partner as best he could, but the accident theory was a shot in the dark at best. Irene sounded like she had ground to stand on, but he still felt the reasoning would crumble if they questioned it.

Digby's cheeks reddened. "And why in God's name would this AB person want to connect Bernadette with Mr. Aston? To what purpose would she have for meddling in these people's lives?"

Irene squared her shoulders. She was switching from defensive mode to fight mode. Joe wasn't going to end their already rocky day with her in trouble for potentially taking a swing at a government agent.

"I don't have enough information to make a valid theory as to why," she finally said. "But when I do, I shall consider contacting you."

Joe made sudden eye contact with Mr. Cullens and his feelings reflected back. This conversation needed to end. He

117

stood up.

"It's been a long day, gentlemen. I think we should call it a night and get to supper."

Mr. Cullens stood as well. "I agree. Please, Miss Holmes, contact us should you have any other information. What you've provided us is quite substantial, indeed, and we thank you greatly for your work. Good evening."

Irene never took her eyes off Digby until Joe escorted both men out of the flat.

He shut the door to the sitting room and sighed. "That could've gone better."

Irene shrugged. "I think it went fine. Though, if Mr. Digby continues to be a problem, then—"

"Then this case will end, and Mr. Cullens will never asked us for help again."

Irene shot him a glare but kept quiet, turning to their board with a finger pressed against her lips.

Chapter VII

Another Visit to the Aston Estate

Irene sat at the wide table in the large back kitchen at Madame Jeannie's brothel. She'd felt fidgety and restless after the day's events. Furthermore, she didn't want to be in the flat alone after Joe left for his date with Sarah, so she dropped in on the Madame for supper.

Most of the others had begun their evenings already, so Irene dined with Nancy, a slight, quiet but cheeky woman, Miriam, a curvy, jovial younger woman, and the Madame herself, whose dark hair was up in rollers as she prepared for her own nightly tasks.

Joe had taken a cab to his date because the Vauxhall was low on petrol; he'd run out of time to fill up the tank before he had to leave. Irene, however, had no such time constraints and gladly filled the petrol tank, then drove herself across the city.

Dinner tonight was sliced ham on thin pieces of bread. She chomped on hers, only half paying attention as Nancy finished telling a scandalous story. Jeannie gave a sharp bark of laughter at the tale's conclusion.

"And that, darlings," she said, the sleeves of her black, fur-trimmed robe draping down to her elbow as she pointed to Nancy, "is why we tie our hair back when dealing with any garment with zippers."

The girls all laughed again. Half of the tales at Madame Jeannie's were enough to make anyone blush, but they never bothered Irene. She didn't understand some of the stories, anyway.

Nancy dug back into her dinner while Miriam let out a sigh, stacking her utensils on her empty plate.

Irene hadn't come here with more of an agenda than eating dinner, but now that her mind was clearing, thoughts about the case came to the forefront.

"I have a question if you all shall indulge me."

"Of course, darling," Jeannie replied with a serene smile.

"Joe and I are in the midst of a tricky investigation. Two people are soon to be married and I cannot figure out why. They are completely mismatched and seem to not suit each other at all."

Miriam smiled as she cleared away the dishes. "Perhaps they are madly in love!"

"Who marries for love anymore?" Nancy snorted as she stood.

The Madame stayed silent for a moment, then turned more serious than Irene had ever seen her. "Nancy makes a good point. Is there something for either of them to gain from this particular bond?"

"None that I can see."

"Ask the bride *how* she fell in love with the groom. Everyone I've met who has been truly in love says that they had a moment of realization where they simply knew that this was the person they'd spend the rest of their life with."

Nancy took Irene's plate and quipped her input. "Some men have that moment a few times a week here."

Both she and Miriam burst out in a fit of giggles.

Jeannie clapped her hands to command their attention. "Girls, off to work! Chop, chop."

The women scampered off.

Irene stared at the dark wall across the room, turning over Madame's words in her mind. She couldn't think of a reason why Timothy and Bernadette would get married unless they were, in fact, in love. But that seemed highly unlikely. Perhaps she didn't dig deep enough into either of them to make that deduction?

Or maybe she just didn't understand what love was.

Which was much more likely.

She knew the love she had for her family and friends, but that was different from romance....

She had no idea what that involved.

Jeannie must've taken Irene's thought process as a pout because she leaned forward and patted Irene's hand.

"Don't worry, love. I'm sure you'll have your moment."

"Oh, I don't think so. I don't even know who I'd have that moment with."

The Madame gave her one of her motherly smiles that stretched right to her eyes. "I'm sure you'll get your moment, Irene Holmes. If you want one, that is."

Then she stood, robes drooping and flowing as she turned to the nearby mirror. She poked at her face and adjusted her hair, fixing a roller that had dropped.

Irene chewed her lip as thoughts rushed through her head at rapid speed.

She and Joe would have to make a trip back to the Aston estate and question Bernadette. Another interview with Timothy would help, too, though she didn't wish to speak to him. However, if it were for the case, she'd chat away like they were old mates. Perhaps they both did have a moment with each other and were genuinely in love.

Other thoughts crept in as well. Would *she* ever have a moment? Did she even want one? She and Joe were doing just fine at Baker Street.

Except it wasn't just the two of them anymore, as he was out many nights with Sarah.

Had they had a moment?

Was a moment even a large matter? Couldn't one simply pick someone who logically suited them and spend their lives with that person?

She scowled at the table, needing to change the subject before she thought circles around herself.

"I am having a New Year's gathering at Baker Street," she said, her words a bit sterner than she meant. "I would love it if you stopped by, Jeannie."

The Madame didn't seem to notice Irene's tone and spun around with a flourish. "Oh, *darling*. I would not miss it! What shall I bring?"

"You don't have to bring anything. I wouldn't even know what to ask you to bring."

Jeannie waved her off. "I shall find something. We're always gifted so lovely around this time of year. It's funny the things men will do to justify what they seek when they come here."

"Wonderful. When I figure out the details, I shall ring you."

The Madame's smile stayed on her face as she approached, grasping Irene's hands.

"It was lovely seeing you tonight, darling. You did seem thoughtful for the whole evening, but it was good you got out."

"Yes, it was," Irene agreed, but her words didn't sound convincing.

"Pardon my saying so, but you look simply exhausted. Go home and get some sleep."

Irene nodded and headed to the back door for her coat and hat. As she dressed, a young woman came into the kitchen, presumably for a break from her work this evening. She gave a small wave, then filled a glass with water.

As Irene tugged her gloves on, the smell of cologne drifted to her nose. It smelled similar to Joe's. She felt her ears heat up.

Much too quickly, she pushed open the door and stepped out

into the cold, damp air, taking deep breaths, trying to clear her nose of the scent.

She'd enjoyed the smell of Joe's cologne when he'd first started wearing it. As soon as he'd starting seeing Sarah, however, he wore the scent every time he would go out that it became a sign that he would be away and not return until Irene was tucked into bed.

By the time she reached her car out on the street, she had rid her nose of the wretched scent. She didn't want to let those thoughts drown out the nice dinner.

As she climbed into the car, though, Irene pouted for a moment before starting the engine. Perhaps she'd find Joe a scent that she enjoyed for when he stayed in, or wore specifically while working their cases. Then her Pavlovian response would shift from one of sour thoughts, to one of glee whenever she caught a whiff of him.

*   *   *   *   *

The rain glistened off the windshield and the streetlights bounced off each drop. As enjoyable as dinner with Jeannie and the ladies had been, Irene was eager to get home, have a bath, and climb into bed. Perhaps she would dig out a book from Joe's pile to soothe her mind for sleep.

She turned left and absentmindedly noted that the car behind her had done the same. London was a busy city, so she didn't concern herself too much. But then the same headlights flashed when she made another turn.

She pushed the pedal, speeding up, and changed lanes, then turned quickly down a smaller side road. A flurry of honks followed, but Irene kept her speed. It took a moment, but there the car was again.

Heart in her throat, she tried to get a better view of her follower, but the headlights shone right in her eyes every time she looked back.

The Vauxhall roared onto a busy street. Irene nearly sideswiped a bus, narrowly missing the towering side panel. She risked a glance and saw her follower fly onto the road, squeezing between two other automobiles.

Irene drove steadily alongside the bus, debating her two options: she could lose the tail by going all over London or she could let herself get caught.

There was enough petrol and more than enough time to race around London to escape whoever was in that car.

On the other hand, curiosity clawed and wouldn't let up. Who was chasing her? What did they want? Did they mean to harm her or deliver a message?

Everyone stopped at a traffic light and Irene twisted in her seat. She attempted to pick out her follower among the sea of headlights but could only see dark shapes, none of which stood out.

When the light turned green, she travelled along with the crowd, occasionally glancing back. Nothing was out of place. She sighed, whether out of disappointment or relief, she didn't know, and headed back to Baker Street.

She turned onto a less busy road and settled into the sparse traffic. The roar of an engine sounded from behind. Irene looked back in time to see headlights growing as they approached.

She cried out in frustration at her persistent pursuer and turned the wheel sharply, the car veering toward the pavement. Her two left-side tires bounced onto the curb, jarring her spine.

A large dark car sped past her, then slid sideways with wheels cocked, attempting to stop. Irene turned the wheel again, getting the Vauxhall off the curb. She did a U-turn and sped the opposite way, honks from others on the road filling the air.

Whoever her pursuer was, they had nearly crashed into her,

meaning they definitely meant harm.

She gripped the steering wheel tight as she manoeuvred the Vauxhall through the road, taking a sharp left, then a right.

The street was full of shops, all closed for the evening, but every other one had a rocky, cobblestone laneway that cut through to the parallel street. Irene came upon a bakeshop and cut down the alleyway, car bouncing along the uneven ground. She flew out the other end and did another left-right combination.

Finally, she stopped the car alongside the curb, just outside a small park. Her knuckles were white from clenching them around the wheel.

Irene sat in silence, chest heaving, eyes searching for her tail.

She must've sat there for at least ten minutes, waiting for a car to either appear from somewhere or suddenly crash into her.

When neither happened, she blew out a breath, attempting to calm her racing heart. She patted the Vauxhall's dashboard, praising the car for keeping together throughout the chase.

She'd ended up down near Convent Garden, at least a fifteen-minute drive from Baker Street. She waited one more moment, then headed north.

As she drove, she was still on high alert, but nothing jumped out as she approached Baker Street. No headlights roared into view.

Her heart raced in her chest again, but this time from excitement. Obviously, she and Joe were close to cracking this case. Otherwise, the orchestrator behind it, -which she was sure was AB- wouldn't have felt the need to send an attacker.

*　　*　　*　　*　　*

She finally made it back to 221B, parking in the spot out front, but waited for a moment, assuring she hadn't been followed. Once she was confident that she was alone, Irene hurried upstairs.

Joe wasn't home yet, but she barely thought about him as she wrote on the board. It wasn't much to go off of, but Madame Jeannie's insight had provided a new course of action for Irene to take with this case.

She didn't make note of what happened in the car, knowing that just the thought of her involvement in an almost fatal crash would rattle Miss Hudson and worry Joe to no end.

She stepped back and took in the board as a whole. Her

fingers tingled as a smile spread across her face.

This case was almost closed.

And hopefully, the visit to the Aston estate tomorrow would give her the final clues.

*   *   *   *   *

The next morning, Irene was still a bit shaken from the night before, if only because that was the body's natural response to a threat, but she was more intrigued than concerned. Who had been following her? Were they trying to hurt or kill her or simply attempting to scare her? Either way, they failed on all accounts because now she knew she was on the right track and wanted more than ever to pursue this case.

As Joe and she ate their breakfast, she still thought it wise to keep silent about the incident. Her roommate seemed happy enough as he read the morning paper and ate his meal.

"We have to go back to the Aston estate today," she broke the silence, finally stabbing some eggs. "I want to ask Bernadette a few more questions about her engagement with Timothy."

Joe frowned. "That didn't go so well last time. You said she seemed to be repeating some script in her head."

"But I want to come at it from a different angle this time."

"We'll need some petrol for the car."

"I put some in last night before I went to Jeannie's."

"You went out last night?"

Joe seemed wary and concerned, presumably because it had been a long while since Irene had gone anywhere by herself – especially at night when she was usually home pondering a case with Joe or staying in the flat by herself.

"Just to Jeannie's for dinner."

"I had no idea," he said, his eyes going wide.

"You should've noticed. Our automobile was parked five feet forwards than when you left."

"It was late when I arrived home. I must have missed that *small* detail."

"Hm."

Irene finished off her eggs.

Joe used to practice his deduction skills and had almost made an obsession at trying to best her, but lately, he hadn't even attempted to make any sort of complex deducing. It was as if he'd given up even trying to match her.

Irene took a large gulp of her juice to distract her mind from those thoughts, then she stood to prepare for their drive out to the Aston Estate.

*   *   *   *   *

Irene, Joe, and Bernadette stood on a balcony overlooking the grand ballroom. Workers scurried below, testing different seating arrangements, looking up at the bride for either a thumbs up or thumbs down, as if she were a Roman emperor judging executions.

Intuition told Irene that the woman *was* orchestrating an execution, she just didn't know what kind.

Bernadette gave a thumbs up for whatever set-up the workers had finished, then turned to the pair of investigators with a polite smile.

"My apologies. It's mere weeks before the ceremony, and I feel like I need to oversee everything."

"Quite alright," Irene replied, watching the woman like a hawk. She seemed much more confident than the previous visit.

Irene was desperate to know *why*. She did another sweep of the woman but still only noted a small dusting of flour on the side of her dress and a few petals from a thistle on the hem of

132

her skirt.

The woman spoke again. "Francine said you wished to talk about how I met Timothy?"

"Sort of," Irene said, paying close attention how she would react to the next question. "I was curious as to when you knew Mr. Aston was the one you'd want to spend the rest of your life with?"

From her peripherals, she saw Joe give her a brief questioning look. She hadn't told him her plans before their trip because it didn't matter what his thoughts were on them. Irene only needed Bernadette's reaction.

The woman in question stared for a moment before answering. "When he asked me to marry him."

"You didn't know before then? There was no moment of realization that this could be the man you wanted to spend the rest of eternity with?"

Reiteraterating Jeannie's words must've touched a sore spot because Bernadette fidgeted, her confidence wavering.

"I suppose it was a few months after we began seeing each other. I just knew. That's it. Timothy loves me, Miss Holmes. Don't think he doesn't."

"Oh, I don't doubt it. But you seem like such an odd pairing that I can't help but wonder what draws you to each other."

Bernadette's cheeks went red, but Irene suspected it wasn't from embarrassment. The woman's face twisted into a glare.

"*You two* don't seem right for each other. A doctor paired with a common busybody. But alas, here you are in my home accusing me of not being in love with the person I am marrying in a few weeks."

Joe stepped up, attempting to calm the situation. "We are truly sorry—"

Irene didn't let him speak, determined to get some kind of answer from Bernadette. "I am not accusing you of anything. I'm simply asking why you want to marry this particular man."

"Because I love him! That should be enough."

"It should, indeed. But when did you fall in love?"

"I don't have time for this. Francine!"

A young maid scurried around the corner, and Bernadette gestured to Irene and Joe. "Escort these investigators out, please."

Then, she turned with a shaky breath and headed in the opposite direction, down a set of stairs leading to the ballroom.

Francine's short figure led Irene and Joe back through the house, aiming for the front door.

"Does Bernadette cook in the kitchen occasionally?" Irene asked as they walked down a long hallway at the front of the house. "I noticed flour stuck to her dress."

The maid's cheek reddened. "I must get that off as soon as I go back. She doesn't cook, nor should she have to, but she is trying to make a dessert."

"What kind of dessert? Something for the wedding?"

"Oh, goodness no," the maid said, as if offended that Irene even had such a thought. "A simple cake. She said that even though she has us to cook and bake, she should keep up her skills by baking a cake recipe passed down from her mother."

"Jolly good." Irene tried to sound interested, but her words came out more suspicious.

They headed past a hallway of offices. As they approached the large oak doors on the right, Timothy and a servant exited the room. He frowned when he saw them.

"Miss Holmes. I didn't know you were back here."

"We were just leaving. Wedding plans seemed to be coming along nicely."

The man shrugged. "All I have to do is show up at the ceremony."

Irene smiled, but knew Timothy saw right through it. "I have a question for you, though. Why did you propose to Bernadette? I know we discussed this earlier, but I would like to know what about her made you know she was the one."

The servant cleared his throat and backed away from the conversation. Francine followed suit, adjusting her position to stand back against the wall, giving them enough space to discuss such a seemingly private matter.

"She's everything I've been looking for, I suppose." Timothy sighed. "You couldn't build me a better-suited woman. She likes what I like, dislikes what I can't stand. She's a little on the mousey side, but it was as if God created her just for me."

Irene felt her eyes narrow. She had to work to keep her face from creating a suspicious expression. It was odd that someone whose husband had just died and became engaged so quickly afterwards seemed to fit someone like Timothy so well.

"Wonderful," she said, attempting her best smile. "Oh, before you go, Joe noticed a wonderful football trophy in the cabinet. Is that yours?"

A grin broke out over Timothy's face, and he looked at Joe. "A football man, are you?"

Joe clenched his jaw. She would've felt bad putting him in such an awkward situation, but she had a new goal in mind, and her poor partner would have to suffer for her to achieve it.

"I am," Joe replied. "Never got to play much at university since I was too busy with my studying."

Like the flip of a switch, Timothy reverted back to the student he'd been during the war and clasped Joe on the back.

"Come here, I'll show you my pride and joy."

A small bench that was probably for decoration only sat across from the office door. Irene plunked down on the soft cushion, crossing her legs and dropping her purse at her feet as if exasperated.

"I shouldn't have said anything," she sighed at Francine, who gave her a curt nod.

Meanwhile, she stared at the office door, left slightly ajar from Timothy's football distraction.

Francine hadn't noticed, or else the maid would've rushed to shut it, but Irene focused on it, eager to get into the room and look around.

But first, the maid had to go.

"You're more than welcome to go brush the flour from Bernadette's dress. I have a feeling these men are going to have a lengthy chat."

Francine shook her head. "I am quite fine here. I'll walk you

137

out when they are done."

Irene groaned inwardly. Poor Joe had only so much false conversation in him before he would need to escape. And she was desperate to get into that office.

"We will really be alright escorting ourselves out. The door is only down the hall. I would hate for you to get into trouble on our account. Bernadette seemed like she was in a particular mood today, what with all the wedding planning and the nerves she must feel. It wouldn't do for her to notice the flour, or worse, transfer it to some other important garment."

Those words piqued Francine's panic, who hesitated a moment, shuffling her feet on the spot. "Perhaps I'd better go..."

Irene gave her a reassuring smile. When the maid finally scampered off, Irene headed for the office door.

Slipping into the room, she pulled the camera from her bag. She intended to keep it for as long as she could get away with as it provided essential services when it came to rifling through people's belongings.

She crouched beside the desk, examining the drawers to attempt to figure out which one housed the important documents.

A key stuck out of the top drawer, and Irene hesitated.

Surely, Timothy wouldn't leave it there if he had his personal belongings, would he?

She pulled the drawer open. Sitting right on top was the will he must've been recently perusing. Irene simply shook her head.

No wonder Mr. Barnes didn't want Timothy running the company.

She snapped a couple of pictures of the piece of paper, tempted to read through the will but knew that it was a risk. Once the photos developed, she'd take a better look at what it said. She tucked the papers back, closing the drawer and ensuring the key was in the exact same place – not that Timothy would notice.

Irene slipped back into the hallway. She heard Joe and Timothy talking about some football match from before the war. As soon as Joe spotted her round the corner, he waved.

"So sorry, Timothy. Duty calls, as they say!"

"No bother, old chap. When this whole investigation mess is over with, you should come by for a game of footy."

"Of course!" Joe said politely, then caught up to Irene.

She gave Timothy a small wave and hurried toward the front door.

They burst out into the cool air, both blowing out steamy

breaths.

"That was rather unpleasant," Joe remarked flatly. "I hope you accomplished what you set out to do."

"I most certainly did," Irene said with a slight grin.

"Good." Joe gave her a curt look, tugging his coat tighter. "Because I exhausted every ounce of football knowledge I had. The only reason that I convinced him I knew what I was talking about was because he simply likes hearing himself speak."

She chuckled as she stepped onto the slick cobblestone laneway. It was then that something caught her eye near the guest garage.

"One moment, Joe."

A thistle bush, overgrown and brown from the cold, sat tucked beside the garage's small side door. Irene crouched beside it. Footprints that were the same size as Bernadette's were just visible in the frozen dirt. She heard Joe walk over, but barely paid attention as questions swirled in her mind.

Why did Bernadette enter the guest garage? What was in there that she needed? Irene couldn't imagine the young bride leaving the property for any reason, and she hadn't mention travelling.

Irene straightened and tried the doorknob, but it didn't

140

budge.

No matter. These types of locks were always straightforward and easy to gain access to. She pulled two pins from her hair, straightening them before jamming them into the lock. A brief moment later, the door opened.

Pulling a torch from her purse, Irene shone a light around the empty garage. A car was covered in a tarp. There were bits and bobs of various automobile parts, along with furniture and antiques one would expect in an old garage.

Right near the door, however, were three cans of antifreeze. Irene kneeled to study the label. There was no thin layer of dust covering the cans like everything else in the room. She dug out her camera for a photo. It might not turn out the clearest, but even a blurred, grainy picture would remind her of what she discovered.

Joe stepped into the garage, but she stood and shooed him out.

"We're done," Irene said, closing the door behind them once they'd stepped back outside. "We must leave before someone spots us rifling through places we shouldn't be."

Chapter VIII

An Especially Horrid Time at the Library

Joe sat at the dining table, turning the teacup in his hands. Irene was upstairs, in the windowless third-floor lavatory, developing the photos from earlier. The tension between them was still a bit high; it bothered Joe that he couldn't pinpoint exactly what was wrong or do anything to solve it.

Today, though, had felt more normal than the past week. Their conversation and synchronicity was still disjointed, but Joe felt, for the first time in a while, that he and Irene were resolving whatever had come between them.

Speak of the devil, she thumped down the stairs and burst into the sitting room, half a dozen photos in her hands. Joe leaned forward across the table as she slid into the dining chair, ready to view them with her. The pictures appeared to be of pieces of paper. Irene held one up, in particular, catching his attention.

"I don't remember you taking this," she said in a playful tone.

Joe smiled at the photo of her outside the Aston estate, on top of the garden's low brick wall. Her hands were on her hips as she surveyed the area.

"I don't have any photos of you."

"So, you chose to capture this moment? I look like a pirate captain on the bough of a ship."

Joe laughed and took the photo. "If that doesn't describe you, then I don't know what would."

Irene scowled, but the grin stayed on her face.

Joe set the photo to the side and poked through the rest of the pile. He sighed as he shuffled through the pictures.

"Are you allowed to take photos of someone's will without their permission?"

"Probably not. But Mr. Aston, the genius that he is, left them in the top drawer of his desk with the key in the lock. It was practically begging to be opened."

Joe smiled despite himself. There was the Irene he knew.

He gestured to the photos. "What does the will say?

Anything of importance?"

Irene skimmed it, then shrugged. "Nothing we don't already know. Timothy is, in fact, leaving the company to Bernadette if he dies. Which we know is purely to spite Mr. Barnes. It appears she gets everything unless they have children. Then, it goes to them."

"So, she will have full control over the company?"

"Yes. I wonder if Mr. Barnes knows that."

"If he does," Joe paused, "could that put Bernadette in some sort of danger? Should we look at it from that angle?"

"But what would Mr. Barnes have to gain from harming her?" Irene furrowed her brows. "I don't think he's even met the woman. My other curiosity is the anti-freeze in the garage."

"And even more curious is why Bernadette appears to be the one who stored it there." Joe stood and collected their empty dishes from the table, thinking aloud as he wandered to the counter. "Could it be to keep some mechanism of hers from freezing?"

"What type of mechanism?"

Joe sat back at the table. "I don't know."

Irene stood. "I am going to ponder the case."

"Don't ponder too long. We're going to the library tonight."

144

"We shall be at the library in good time. Don't worry."

Joe watched as Irene scooped a pillow from the couch and dropped it on the floor by the Christmas tree. She laid down, head on the pillow, tucked halfway under the tree like a present. She closed her eyes, clasped her hands over her stomach, and... pondered.

In the meantime, Joe gathered the photos into a pile. "Perhaps Bernadette and Timothy are simply in love, and there is no grand mystery."

Irene snorted. "What is the point of love?"

He knew she'd asked the question rhetorically, but answered anyway: "Love can be wonderful. My parents were madly in love and still are. They make each other happier every day."

Irene was silent for so long, almost as if she'd fallen asleep.

Or perhaps she was simply ignoring him, which was completely plausible.

But, after another silent moment, she asked him a question.

"Have you ever been in love?"

He stared at her, but her eyes remained closed. The question blindsided him. Even though he thought about his answer, his head was already shaking *No*. Between schooling, his practice and the war, his free time was minimal.

Sarah was the first women he'd dated with any serious intent. And he certainly wasn't in love with her yet. At least, he didn't think so.

"No. I haven't."

He thought about asking her the same question but reconsidered. Irene would scoff and lecture him about how love was pointless, and he simply wasn't up for that at this particular moment.

"I have to wonder what being in love is even like."

Again, she caught him off-guard. Joe felt the need to answer if only to confirm his own ideals in his mind. He stood from the table to put the photos away.

"I assume it's like being best friends," he began, remembering his mum and dad and their daily interactions with each other. "It's knowing you're going to spend the rest of your life with one person and being thrilled at the thought. It's being completely enraged but knowing you'd still do anything for them. It's laughing at the stupid things they do and having jokes that only the two of you know. It's being a team and having your own little world that, from the outside, may look a little crazy to others but is safe and sound to you both..."

He trailed off as he attempted to think of more, but when it appeared like Irene wasn't listening again, he walked to the file cabinet under their board. As he tucked the photos into the file they'd started, she gave a thoughtful harrumph from the ground.

"That can't be it, Joe," she said dismissively. "You've just described *our* relationship."

Joe froze, file in his hand, half bent towards the small cabinet. He *had* just described them.

He became awkward and nervous all at once as he tried to rid his head of any thoughts that would lead him down that path.

Irene, however, did it for him.

"Maybe there is no such thing as love, and it's all just in everyone's heads."

He looked at her then, but she had retreated back into her mind, shuffling even further under the tree. Instead of replying, he wandered to his chair with his latest novel. He needed a complete distraction until they headed out to the library for Sarah's get-together.

*   *   *   *   *

The early evening air was chilly. As Joe and Irene walked down the pavement to the large library steps, he tugged his jacket tighter. He didn't know why, but this particular winter was hitting him harder than any previous had. He was constantly cold, which irked him. Perhaps it was merely because he was doing more outdoor activities this season. In the past, he'd stay inside and tend to his practice or spend the winters helping his mother with their jams.

Irene had wanted him to drive because she 'simply wasn't in the mood to be behind the wheel'. He wasn't quite sure what that meant but had taken the keys anyway.

They reached the library, and Joe let out a nervous breath. He was glad his partner was here, whether she was particularly thrilled or not.

As they approached the building, she stopped at the steps and put her finger to her lips in thought.

"This timeline is tricky."

"What?" Joe looked around at the building, then the road, to see if he missed something she'd noticed.

Irene stared down at the pavement in thought. That's when Joe realized she was talking about the case. He glanced at the doors and took a step toward them, encouraging her to follow. When she didn't move, he stepped back down beside her.

"Must we discuss this right now?"

"I've been thinking about it as we walked," she said, seemingly ignoring him, "and it appears to be random events, but if strung together, perhaps they make sense."

"Irene," Joe sighed. "I really don't want to be late."

She ignored him again and paced at the bottom of the steps. "Bernadette's husband is killed, then someone tries to kill Timothy. Then, the two of them meet and are engaged. Bernadette has anti-freeze in her garage, and Timothy has left his entire fortune to his future bride. Now, if she wanted to kill him, that's one thing, but what does she have to gain from having his fortune? She doesn't seem to be power-hungry, nor does like she particularity like living in the Aston estate."

Joe threw his hands in the air. "Perhaps she just likes killing her husbands!"

She turned to him, her eyebrow raised. "That makes no sense, Joe."

He stepped up to her, towering over her. "It doesn't matter if it makes sense, Irene. I'm sorry, but we are not working on the case at this moment. We are about to go to a lovely gathering that we've been invited to, and I am a little nervous."

"Nervous?" Irene looked past him to the library as if the building held some answers. "Why are you nervous? You've been seeing Sarah for almost two months."

"But these are Sarah's friends." He felt his stomach turn at the notion of meeting new people and attempting to impress them. "I have to do my best to not embarrass myself and to make a good impression."

She sighed, and Joe nearly turned and walked into the building himself. She had a very combative look about her: eyebrows furrowed and shoulders were stiff and square.

"Why should you impress them? If Sarah likes you, which she does, then what does it matter if other people do?"

"Because that's just what happens in the real world," Joe retorted, and he knew this conversation would take a dangerous turn if they kept arguing. "Can we please discuss the case later?"

"Later?" Irene's eyes went wild for a moment as if Joe's words hit a trigger. "When will 'later' be, Joe? It can't be later tonight because we are here, about to go into that building and discuss... God knows what. We could resume the case tomorrow, but what if Sarah wants to go for breakfast, or what if Eddy pops in, or Miss Hudson has to do her cleaning and interrupts us? We need to use every minute we have to solve this before time runs out and someone else dies. AB is planning a murder, and I must figure it out. And for that, I need time."

By the end of her speech, her chest was heaving, and Joe noticed her clenched fists. Her words went much deeper than this case and housed some underlying issues that he wanted to help with, but he simply had no idea how. He was already a bundle of nerves walking through the door, and he'd hoped that having Irene by his side would soothe him as he met with Sarah's friends, but if she was in such a mood, then the night would end in disaster.

He didn't want to say the next few words out loud, but this conversation needed to end so the night can move on, with or without Irene.

"If you want to work on the case, then go home and do that."

For a moment, Irene's eyes went wide. She looked briefly hurt, which crushed Joe's heart. He opened his mouth to apologize, but she spoke, recovered already.

"To be by myself for another night? No, thank you."

He felt his fingers curl and his jaw clenched. He had no idea what to do now. Usually, he could handle Irene, but not tonight. He remembered how he thought they were back to their normal selves, but the night was full of bumps, which he didn't know how to smooth.

"Then I don't know what you want. If *I* stay at the house,

then I am miserable, but if I leave, *you* are miserable. When you come with me, you are sullen and rude, but if I leave you behind, I feel guilty. We need to think of a solution because this is exhausting. Now, I want to go to the library and see Sarah and her friends, and I want to enjoy myself. You can come with me, which I would love, or you can take the car back to Baker Street. Either way, decide now because I am walking up these steps."

In the sunset light, Irene's dark eyes glowered up at him. It contrasted the lovely make-up she wore and the blue hat her curls peeked out from. It was a look that could kill a man if weaponized.

Joe stood frozen like a statue.

She took a deep breath, never breaking eye contact, then squared her shoulders and marched up the steps, all grace and poise. He followed, exhausted.

The night had only just begun.

*   *   *   *   *

Joe heard the small crowd chattering and laughing as soon as he stepped into the far side of the library where the meeting rooms were. About two dozen people stood around, sipping tea, some holding books, all of them smiling. He felt both nervous and at ease all at once. All these people were like him. They all enjoyed reading and discussing literature. Sarah was wearing a lovely red dress, which made him smile. Her hair was done up similar to Irene's, and she seemed to light up the room, especially compared to his roommate's glower.

Joe gave his head a small shake. He needed to cease comparing everyone to Irene and simply enjoy the evening. Sarah caught his eyes and hurried over. She wrapped her arms around his neck, squeezing tight.

"I'm so glad you made it! You too, Irene! Come, both of you. You'll have such a good time!"

She skipped away from them back towards the crowd. Joe looked to Irene – as he often did in situations where they both stuck out like sore thumbs – but she didn't reciprocate the look. Instead, she strode forward and headed to a smaller crowd that appeared to be discussing palaeontology or archaeology.

He sighed, then reminded himself that he was here for Sarah. Irene was an adult and could handle herself.

"Joe!" his girlfriend called, waving at him. He nodded an acknowledgement and headed over to the group she stood with.

*   *   *   *   *

Almost two hours later, Joe had settled in with Sarah's friends who were chatting about upcoming book releases they were quite excited for. The woman in question had her arm tucked through his, and every now and then, she'd give his bicep a squeeze.

For the first time in a while, he was relaxed and enjoying an activity that was outside the realm of his investigative friend and the cases they solved. Sarah's friends asked about the investigations, of course, and he attempted to make them sound as exciting as possible with the least amount of words.

Meanwhile, Irene stayed to her side of the gathering. Joe knew that if he spoke of their adventures too much, she'd come over to either correct him or add her own opinion.

About half an hour before, a rather loud individual who'd gone to university with a few of Sarah's friends arrived at the gathering. He seemed slightly inebriated, throwing his opinions around quite aggressively. Joe had kept half an eye on him as he made the rounds to the different groups. He was just rechecking the man's position when Sarah tapped his arm.

"Glen is fine. He's just a little opinionated, but he wouldn't hurt a fly."

A man named Mickey, who sat across from Sarah, slapped his knee. "Once you get a taste of investigation, you're suspicious of everyone, it seems."

The group chuckled. Joe laughed along with them, but worry still stirred in his belly. If that man ended up at Irene's group, she'd put him in his place quick...

He stole a glance at her. She wasn't smiling. Her eyes kept skimming over everyone's outfit at her little group of five, yet she didn't look tense or ready to flee.

Sarah asked him a question about the science fiction novel he'd recently finished, which took his attention. He happily jumped into the technology in the story before Glen, the loud gentleman, spoke the most horrid and frightening sentence ever.

"I find most of the Sherlock Holmes stories to be nothing more than drivel. That Watson fellow probably embellished them for print anyway."

Joe felt his blood run cold. Before his mind could register, he rushed toward Irene's group. Sarah called his name, but he ignored her, squeezing through two people on a direct route to prevent whatever catastrophe was about to occur.

155

As he approached the group, his partner's cold voice cut through the rest of the conversation.

"What did you just say about Sherlock Holmes?"

Joe's legs couldn't move fast enough. He faintly heard Sarah call his name again, but his focus was on Irene. He arrived in time to see the woman wind her fist back.

"I'm simply saying," Glen didn't leave well enough alone, "some of the stories seem a little far-fetched, and Holmes himself seems a dreadful person and impossible for anyone to like—"

Irene punched the man right in the nose. He dropped like a bag of rocks.

Gasps flew through the small group. Joe grabbed Irene's shoulders before she could surge forward to get another hit in. Blood oozed from Glen's nose, but he wasn't unconscious. He shakily got to his feet, hand covering his face.

"What the *hell* was that for?" He roared, then he rounded on Joe. "Keep control of your woman!"

"We are terribly sorry," Joe stuttered, cheeks hot with embarrassment.

"*I* am not sorry," Irene spat over his shoulder. "I should've knocked you out, but I was being gracious."

By now, everyone had gathered around. Among the crowd, Sarah was holding her hand over her mouth in shock.

Joe needed to remove Irene from the library before she picked a fight with everyone who looked sideways at her.

"We're going to go."

She fought back, her eyes shooting daggers at everyone. "I think I'll stay and keep discussing more of my father's cases."

More gasps flew around, causing Joe to groan. Now was not the time nor place to start announcing to the world what her connection was to the famous detective.

"Oh, sorry," Irene continued, sarcasm and smugness dripping from every word. "Did I not introduce myself before? I am Irene *Holmes.*"

The gasps turned to murmurs. Irene began to shake. Joe could practically see the adrenaline coursing through her lithe frame. Her fists were still clenched, ready to strike out again.

He got a firm hold on her arm and waist and used a good amount of force to spin her around.

Embarrassment didn't even begin to describe what he was feeling. He felt sick to his stomach as he dragged the angry detective away from the party. She fought him the entire time, like a toddler about to throw a temper tantrum, digging in her

157

heels.

On the way past the coat rack, he roughly grabbed her jacket, sending the hanger flying through the air.

By the time they made it to the lobby, Irene had stumbled beside him, attempting to keep up with his long strides. Joe still kept a firm grasp on her arm, not daring to release her until they were a safe distance away. He shouldered the front door open. A blast of cold air hit them as they exited.

As soon as they were out, Irene twisted out of his grasp and stumbled down the front steps of the building. Her chest heaved. She looked everywhere but at Joe, attempting to find a target for her anger.

Joe's own fists were balled, his chest tightened in rage. He felt his face heat up as he tossed her her coat and pointed to the street.

"Put this on and go to the car."

She seemed momentarily surprised by his anger but pulled her eyes into a glare and spun on her heel, marching down the pavement. Joe stalked behind her, fuming, and swore he felt smoke coming from his ears.

Irene folded her arms across her chest, waiting for him to unlock the car. He opened the passenger door up and slammed it as soon as she was in the seat.

As he stomped around to the driver's side, he coughed, trying to ease the tension in his chest. He begged the panicked episode to stay away – at least until they got home.

"What the *hell* were you doing?" he snapped as he got into the car and reached for the engine switch. "You thoroughly embarrassed me in there. And Sarah. I can't even begin to comprehend what you were thinking."

Irene stared forward, out the windshield, a pout in her lips as her gaze shot daggers into the dark.

"Is this you for the night, then?" he continued. When she still didn't answer, he started the car and muttered as he pulled away from the curb. "How do I go back there and pretend like you didn't just break someone's nose in the middle of the library?"

As Joe wove through the dark streets of London, he felt more and more words working their way to the surface. They were halfway home when his thoughts finally bubbled over.

"I saw this coming. I saw this outburst building up in you, and I should've said something. Not that you would've talked to me about it anyway. I have been nothing but an open book, but to get anything from you is the most difficult thing I've had to

159

do. Every time you get into a mood, we go through the same thing, Irene. I don't know what more I have to do to show you that I am here for you. That you can trust me."

Sudden tiredness swept over him, and he slumped his shoulders. Irene's features flashed every other second in the streetlights; she hadn't moved a muscle.

After a moment, Joe heard her take a ragged breath, and he looked at her. She stared at her lap, fingers clawing at her knees as if moving that slight amount would release whatever emotions she felt. It was a moment before she spoke at last.

"Clearly, I am not dealing with anything well at this particular time." Her voice was stiff, as if she was holding back a flood of emotional tears. "I have more friends now than I've ever had, yet I feel the most alone. Everyone is moving on with their lives, leaving me behind, and the silly thing is, I have nowhere to go even if I wanted to. There is no place for me to move forward to. And there is no one to move forward with."

Her words pricked Joe's heart.

"You and I are moving forward together."

She shook her head. "You are moving forward with your friends. With Michael, and now with Sarah. Eddy has been promoted, so he will have even less time than usual. There is no

160

place for me."

Joe stopped at a red light and took the chance to close his eyes for a second. *This* was an underlying issue with Irene, and he'd noticed it about a month ago. He had had no idea what to do about it then, and still didn't now.

"Let me be there for you, Irene. Let me take some of that burden and help you figure out what to do to change that feeling."

She flinched as if his offer physically hurt her. When she spoke, she was defensive with her words.

"It is not your issue. I don't need help from anyone, and I don't intend to be a bother."

Joe felt his frustration mounting and gripped the steering wheel hard as he drove.

"You are my friend. My dear friend and flatmate. I care about you and any issues you have, and if I can help you, then I want to."

She glared out the windshield again, folding her arms in a pout. Joe's frustration with this night erupted then. He'd dealt with her pouts and her mood swings, and he thought he had a pretty decent handle on her, but this night was exhausting and stressful enough without Irene's involvement.

"Fine," he finally snapped. "Sit there and pout. Retreat inwards and stay that way forever. You pretend like you have no feelings when, in reality, you are more emotional than anyone I know. The more you try to bury them and deal with all the trauma alone, the more unstable you grow. You're not the only one who has endured hardships, Irene. We all have a packed bag we carry around, and some of us are actively trying to empty it. You have the opportunity to help yourself. You have people who care. But you don't allow yourself any kind of reprieve."

He paused to take a deep breath, sweat beading on his forehead.

Irene shook in the seat, and the streetlights caught the tears welled in her eyes, threatening to fall.

"Pull over," she snapped. When he didn't react in an instant, she raised her voice. *"Stop the damn car."*

Joe quickly pulled to the curb and peeled his hands from the steering wheel. He was shaking with adrenaline and frustration, but a small part of him was glad he wasn't driving, as this whole conversation was a heavy distraction from the dangerous winter roads.

He took another deep breath and felt himself slowly calming.

Irene opened the door and climbed out of the car.

For a fraction of a second, he stared at the empty seat, his mouth agape, before scrambling to open his own door.

"Stop! Where are you going?"

"Walking the rest of the way." She stood on the pavement, hand on the open car door.

"We are three blocks from home. Get in the car. We can finish the conversation back at Baker Street."

Irene shook her head and shut the door, stepping away. A tear rolled down her cheek.

"Go back to Sarah," she sneered. "She needs more attention paid towards her, as she often looks at me like I may pounce on you to stake my claim."

With that, she turned and walked away.

"Irene!" Joe shouted, his cheeks warm in embarrassment and anger. He killed the engine and quickly followed.

She'd made it about twenty feet before he grabbed her arm.

"Stop."

Irene spun around, looking up at him with raging dark eyes before wrenching herself away.

"Everyone is going to leave me, Joe." Her voice caught with raw emotion. "Whether it be because they get married, they die, or they just stop caring."

"Everyone is going to leave?" He gestured wildly, incredulous and needing an outlet for all the adrenaline. "Think about all the people you invited to our New Year's party. I don't see them leaving any time soon."

She scoffed and quickly wiped a tear away. "They all have their own people, their own lives. I am nothing but a common thread between them. I do not belong anywhere. I am just here, by myself, using people when I need something from them."

"That's unfair, Irene," Joe said, his voice turning into a low, angry rumble.

"Is it? Everyone is exhausted by me. I see it even when they don't think I do. Everyone scoffs at me, scolds me. No one willingly rings me to go to dinner or the cinema. I force myself upon people until they have no choice but to need me. It's what I did to you. I forced you to live with me and solve crimes when I knew you'd rather be doing something else. Everyone has other people they would rather be with if given a choice. It's becoming quite clear."

Joe shook his head, his stomach turning at her words. He certainly didn't feel that way, but he was too angry to formulate the words.

Irene wiped a final tear before her face became still as a statue. The mask she usually wore, slightly smug and disinterested, settled back into place.

"Tell them whatever you wish when you return to the library. That I've gone mental. I don't care. But you should go back. Sarah will be wondering where you are."

She pulled her jacket tighter and turned on her heel, quickly disappearing into the fog.

Joe watched her go, his arms hanging limp. A small lump formed in his throat, and he had no idea where it came from. He felt like he wanted to cry and punch a wall at the same time. Her words cut deeper than he expected, but he wasn't surprised. He'd seen how she used her words as a weapon; he just never thought she'd turn her aim at him.

He shivered as the wind picked up – he'd left his coat back at the library. The prospect of travelling all the way back there was daunting and made his chest tighten with a whole new panic.

But he had to return and offer some kind of explanation to Sarah, even if he waited outside for her until the party finished.

Joe took one last look down the foggy street, the lump in his throat returning. Swallowing it, he headed back to the car.

Chapter IX

The Incident on the Way Back to Baker Street

Irene felt sick to her stomach. So sick, she paused twice as if to vomit. The moment she was far enough from Joe, she'd let the tears fall. The fog grew thick and the damp air seeped into her clothes, but she didn't care.

A part of her meant every word she'd said, but another was devastated for directing her anger at Joe.

Then, there was the part of her that was genuinely disgusted she'd even spoke any of the thoughts out loud at all.

Despite loathing every word that came out of her mouth, the questions still remained. Who *did* she have? Who actually cared that she was here? If she disappeared, no one's lives would be any different.

These thoughts made her skin itch. She'd been raised by one of the most confident men on this planet, and up until her return to Baker Street, she'd shared that conviction.

Perhaps Joe was right. All her bravado was simply a mask to keep her true feelings at bay. What were her true feelings? Currently, she felt cold and lonely.

Perhaps if she slept on it, everything would be alright in the morning. That's the way it usually went, anyway. They would snip at each other, but in the morning, it was as if nothing had happened.

This fight was different, though, and the nauseous feeling in her stomach reminded her of that as she continued down the slick pavement. Joe had targeted her underlying issues with precise aim. In return, she'd fired her words at his weakest points.

Perhaps Miss Hudson would know what to do.

Irene shuddered at the thought of telling her landlady what she'd said to Joe, deciding to figure out what to do on her own.

The more she walked into the fog, the less she could see in front of her. She dug a handkerchief from her pocket and wiped her dripping nose, shivering at the chill of the cold air against her tear-stained face.

Her deepest desire was to lock herself away for the night and avoid everything and everyone until things sorted themselves

167

out.

Heavy boots sounded from behind, distracting her. Irene slowed to hear better.

The footsteps slowed as well, causing the hair on the back of her neck to prick.

Someone was following her.

She immediately went on high alert, attempting to rid herself of all the weariness.

A shadow moved in front of her. Irene balled her fists, ready to strike out if need be.

She didn't see the dark figure until it was too late.

He shoved her hard, flying into the alley beside her. She grabbed for her purse – and for anything useful inside – but cussed when she remembered she'd left it in the car.

They were in a dead end. With no other choice, Irene turned on the balls of her feet, her fists clenched and up, ready to fight.

Two men entered the alley dressed in heavy coats, hats tugged down, obscuring their faces. The taller one was twice her size, whereas the shorter one had scars decorating his neck and knuckles.

Adrenaline pumped through her veins, and she almost attacked them without thinking. Her anger formed a ball inside, demanding she take her emotions out right now.

"Drop the investigation," the tall man grunted.

Irene simply blinked as if they'd said the most ridiculous thing in the world. "No."

The man hesitated before attempting his threat again. "Drop the case, or things will become very bad for you."

She laughed despite herself, raising an eyebrow. "I assure you, things cannot get worse for me. Go back to your boss and tell her that she is more than welcome to speak to me in person. Now, move before I make you."

The two glanced at each other, and Irene almost laughed again. They were expecting her to give up.

She folded her arms across her chest and tapped her foot but still kept ready for an attack. Hopefully her bluff worked so she could escape this situation without any further hassle.

The tall henchman was prepared to take this meeting one step further.

He reached under his jacket. Irene uncrossed her arms. If he produced a weapon, she'd need to disarm him as quickly as possible. Hand-to-hand she could manage, but there was nothing she could do against a bullet or knife blade.

She leapt forward before he could pull the weapon, her

hands clasping his wrist as it moved. Snapping his wrist, she eyed the small pistol as it flew through the air. The metal skidded across the alley and she breathed a sigh of relief. Without a weapon, she could hold her own.

Irene turned her body, still clutching the man's wrist, digging her shoulder into his chest. She rolled them both onto the ground, releasing him and jumping to her feet. He stayed on the cobblestone, shaking his wrist while he groaned in pain.

The short man made a grab for her, but she jabbed her open-palmed hand into his nose. He stumbled back as blood poured from his face over his fingers.

Simultaneously, the taller man struggled to his feet. Irene kicked out, boot connecting with his face. He dropped to the ground again, howling in pain.

She quickly looked around the alley and spotted the gun next to a dwindling pile of coal. As she rushed to it, a third man appeared. He scooped her up and threw her sideways across the alley. She collapsed in a heap but quickly scrambled to her feet. Not fast enough, however. The man swung, his fist connecting with her face. Irene stumbled into the wall, cheek throbbing, stars in her eyes.

The man swung again, but she dodged, and he hit the wall

instead. He shouted a string of profanities, knuckles cracking as they collided with the bricks. Irene jabbed him twice in the stomach, anger raging through her body. She tried to swing again, but sudden exhaustion swept over her. She faltered, missing her target completely.

Large hands grabbed her from behind. The other men were still out there… She cussed at herself for temporarily forgetting.

She twisted as best she could and locked her ankles behind her attacker's knees, then lurched forward. They both rolled to the ground and she squirmed out of his grasp. The newcomer punched her in the face just as she regained composure.

Irene stumbled, dazed, and a boot connected with her stomach. She doubled over, heaving. Another punch landed as she turned to keep fighting. This time, she dropped to the ground. Warm liquid dripped into her eyes and past her nose to the cold cobblestones. She blinked rapidly, searching some sort of pipe or weapon.

A large hand grabbed her collar, dragging her to her feet. She kicked him hard in the groin, and he released her. Then, she hit him twice in a row and heard something in his cheek snap. He howled in pain and staggered away.

Two left.

One shoved her before she could dodge, then smacked her. Falling to the ground again, she cursed out loud. Her stomach suffered another punch. The man pushed Irene over with his foot, but she grabbed his ankle and yanked him to the ground. Tears and blood streamed down her chin and neck, but she kept going, wrapping her ankles around his neck and rolled them into the middle of the alley.

Heavy hands dragged her to her feet, shoving her face-first into the wall. The brick scraped her already bruising cheek, further splitting whatever wound was above her temple. Irene cried out in pain and tried to kick her foot back but missed everything. The man twisted her arm behind her back and yanked, shoulder threatening to pop from its socket.

She gritted her teeth through the pain.

He pressed his body into hers, breath hot in her ear as he spoke. "Drop the case."

"No!" she growled, her words muffled.

He put pressure on her neck, and Irene cried out in pain again.

"Drop the case. Or next time we see you, you won't make it out alive."

She wanted to retort with something clever, but her pulse

beat so loudly in her ears that she could barely hear anything going on around her, let alone think of something to say.

The man grabbed the back of her jacket and threw her hard into the alley. Irene collapsed on the ground in a heap, the air knocked out of her. She craned her neck to face her attackers again, but the alley was empty.

She spat out a glob of blood. Her whole body felt heavy and weak, her skin tingling. Her face and neck were slick. The air chilled her right to the bone.

She dragged herself to the wall and leaned on the brick for support as she climbed to her feet. Her knees threatened to buckle but stayed locked while she took a few deep breaths.

221B was a three-minute walk away on a good day, but right now, it seemed like it was across the city. Irene gave herself another minute, then slowly shuffled out of the alley, fighting back nausea from her spinning head. She looked up and down the pavement, momentarily disoriented, before recollecting herself.

At one point, just two doors down from her building, she stumbled into a parked automobile. She almost stayed against it, the cool metal slick from the fog, but pushed herself off and continued on.

When she finally reached the front door, her hand slipped several times as she tried to turn the knob. It finally gave, and she crashed inside. The door banged against the wall. Stumbling, Irene made it to the bottom of the stairs, leaning against the wall, chest heaving, body shaking.

She had no idea how loud she was, but it must have been enough to rouse Miss Hudson, who came rushing out.

The woman huffed around the corner, no doubt prepared to chastise Irene for making so much noise. As soon as she saw the state of her, though, she let out a loud gasp and rushed over

"Irene! What on earth happened?!"

Her shrill voice pierced Irene's ears and made her wince.

"To the hospital!"

Irene shook her head. "I... am fine."

"Like hell, you are! Who did this? Where is Joe? *Where is Joe?*"

"He's fine. They just got me."

"Who got you?" Miss Hudson bustled about, grabbing her jacket from the hook. "We'll get you to the hospital, then I will alert Eddy. Stay here while I ring for an ambulance—"

"No," Irene snapped, keeling over as a pain cut through her stomach. "No hospital. Nothing is broken."

"Irene," Miss Hudson warned, "we must—"

"No hospitals. Bad things happen in hospitals."

She slowly laid down on the stairs in such an awkward position, she instantly wished she'd stayed standing.

"We're going and I will not hear any more arguments."

"No!" Irene shouted as loud as her lungs allowed, fresh tears springing to her eyes. She looked at Miss Hudson through blurry, shaking vision. "I will not go to the hospital. Father went to the hospital after his fall and they said he was going mad. Uncle John *died* in a hospital. I will not go!"

A sob escaped Irene's body, and she watched blood drop onto the wooden stairs beneath her. "I will not go..."

She couldn't see what Miss Hudson was doing, but after a moment, she felt the woman's hands under her arms.

"Then let's get you upstairs," the old woman told her. It sounded like she was crying. "I will ring the doctor and tell him to bring all his equipment, then we will clean you up while we wait."

*   *   *   *   *

At first, Irene refused to let Miss Hudson into the lavatory

175

while she washed. The two argued through the door about privacy, half of Irene's words mumbled and tired. Eventually, the housekeeper burst through the door and insisted on scouring every inch of Irene's body to make sure she wasn't missing any pieces.

"This is going to need a stitch or two." Miss Hudson frowned, gently grabbing her head.

"Then I'll get a stitch." Irene winced as she moved her shoulder, the muscle clearly torn. She felt it swelling as she spoke.

Miss Hudson grabbed a large towel from the pile of clean laundry sitting in the basket beside the tub and held it up while Irene stood, her legs still shaky.

"The doctor will be here any moment." The woman wrapped Irene up, then sighed at her face, presumably seeing the bruises that were surely forming.

"I'm sorry, was I supposed to just let them threaten me and get away with it?"

"Yes!" Miss Hudson began to drain the bathwater. "*Of course* you were supposed to let them get away with it."

Irene tugged on pyjamas, needing help with the shirt as her shoulder refused to move without burning in agonizing pain.

She'd told Miss Hudson about walking home and getting attacked in the alley, how the men told her to stop investigating the case. She'd also mentioned that she'd had a small argument with Joe, but couldn't bring herself to admit how nasty the fight had been – mostly because the guilt she felt still ate away at her, along with all the other aches.

By the time Miss Hudson was done with the buttons, Irene was ready to drop at any moment. As the old woman shooed her out of the bathroom, she stumbled across the sitting area.

"Father wouldn't have let them get away with it," Irene mumbled as she manoeuvred through the mess in her bedroom.

Miss Hudson tidied as she followed Irene, scooping up clothes and books.

"Your father kept his skills up, and when you were younger, you did the same. But I haven't seen you do any of that fisticuffs or rolling and tumbling nonsense since being back here. Even the great Irene Holmes needs practice every now and again."

The front doorbell rang. Miss Hudson fluffed Irene's pillows, ensuring that she was sitting up in bed and ready for the doctor, before heading down. Irene watched her go, still feeling like she was swaying. She'd be lucky to stay awake before the doctor made it up the seventeen steps.

177

*   *   *   *   *

The doctor snipped the end of the thread, then tucked the tools back into his bag. Irene struggled to keep her eyes open as he spoke to Miss Hudson.

"Strict bed rest for a week, at least," he said before handing two bottles of pills. "And these. She can't be doing any lifting, or else that shoulder will pop right out."

Irene groaned as she listened. A week? That wouldn't do at all. She opened her mouth to argue, but Miss Hudson was already escorting the man down the stairs, so she sunk back into the pillows. How was she supposed to finish the case? How was she supposed to do *anything*?

Irene winced as a headache sliced through her temples. Perhaps a wee bit of rest *was* necessary right now.

She shifted on the bed, attempting to lay down, and her eyes swept over the pictures on her dresser –the one of her father and Uncle John caught her attention.

A sudden wave of emotion washed up, bringing tears to her eyes. She furiously wiped them away, angry for all the crying she'd done today.

"Why can't you be here?" she snapped at the photo, then a sob wracked her body. "Why can't either of you tell me what to do? Why can't you help me? I miss you both so much..."

Irene realized she hadn't said those words out loud until now.

She wanted Uncle John to stitch her up, give her medication and check on her every hour. He'd fix her without judging how she even came to be in this particular state in the first place. He'd give her a bowl of sweets as he bandaged her, telling her funny stories of his and Father's adventures.

She wanted Father to hug her and tell her she did a good job fighting off those men. To keep pursuing every facet of this investigation. She needed those cakes he brought home that they'd share in front of the fire while tossing different kinds of paper into the flame to see how they burned.

Miss Hudson slipped into the room and sat at the end of the bed, taking Irene's hand. She stayed silent for a few long moments, letting Irene have all the time she needed. When her sobs were under control, she looked at Miss Hudson through puffy eyes.

"How do you do it? How do you see Father week after week? You must be the strongest person I know..."

179

The old woman patted her hand. "My heart breaks every time I see him. But I celebrate the little victories. The small recognition in his eyes when he reads an old letter from John or looks at his pictures of you on the table beside his chair."

A tremor shook through Irene and Miss Hudson squeezed her fingers.

"I don't understand," she replied sadly. "I don't understand why Father's mind went like that. I don't understand why Uncle John was taken. Of all the loathsome people in this world that we'd be grateful were gone, the universe had to take two of the greatest."

"Irene..." The landlady attempted to sound her disapproval at the statement but failed. "We shouldn't talk like that."

"I am correct, though, aren't I? It simply isn't fair."

"Sometimes life deals us a hand we aren't prepared for, and we end up losing a round."

"I do not like things I cannot control. And I don't like losing."

Miss Hudson chuckled, but the smile that came over her face was sad and mournful. "I don't think anyone does, love. I want you to remember something, though. You aren't the only one mourning people you loved. Sherlock and John were just as

180

much my family as yours, and I loved them both dearly. You aren't alone. You have many people that love you and would sit and listen to you should you ever need to talk."

Irene's stomach turned sour and she had to look away. Joe had said practically the same thing in the automobile and she'd brushed him off. Thinking about him made her feel nauseous and anxious. So, for the first time ever, she concentrated on her father instead.

"When I would tell Father that I loved him, he'd say, 'I love you more'. I'd argue that *I* loved *him* more, and he'd tell me that was scientifically impossible. It's the one thing I never sought to research, even as a joke."

Miss Hudson patted her head gently. "You'd find that he was absolutely correct. A parent's love is always the strongest, especially Sherlock's. He doesn't love anything in his life as much as he loves you. And neither did John, and neither do I."

"I love you too, Miss Hudson." Irene sniffled, barely able to keep her eyes open.

The old woman hugged her gingerly. "And you know Eddy and Joe love you too, in their own way."

Hearing his name, Irene had to turn away, ears warming in embarrassment. Her lip trembled as a new wave of tears surged

181

to her eyes.

"I was terrible to Joe, Miss Hudson. I was so *mean*. We had a fight in the middle of the street and I said such nasty things. I don't know if he will ever forgive me."

"I'm sure he will. This is Joe. I know for a fact that he loves you."

Irene shook her head. "I've made him truly angry. He'll never want to speak to me again."

Miss Hudson set her shoulders and looked at her square in the eyes. "Now, you know that's not true. Unless you've suddenly met a completely different Joe than the one I know. Have you?"

Irene shook her head, then winced, tears springing up again. Miss Hudson wiped them away.

"Alright, enough of that," she stated, turning into the stern caretaker again. "You've had a wee dust-up and a row with your friend – nothing to get down in the dumps about. Now, get some sleep. Right now our front hallway looks like one of those crime scenes you frequent. I've got to scrub your blood off the stairs before Joe comes in and has a heart attack."

Irene settled in bed as the old lady left the room, closing the door behind her. She took one last glance at her dresser before slipping into sleep and though she couldn't see the photos clearly through the darkness, a smile came across her face nonetheless.

Chapter X

The Aftermath of a Nasty Row

Joe sat in the automobile staring up at 221B. The lights were off in the main sitting room on the second floor, which didn't surprise him. Irene had most likely gone to bed, for which he was glad. He had no idea what more he could say to her. Tomorrow's breakfast would be dreadful.

There had been a lot of smoothing over to do with Sarah. He had waited outside the library for almost forty minutes before she finally emerged. Joe had apologized, and they had a long talk about the boundaries he needed to set for Irene.

It was the same talk they had every week about her seemingly complete dismissal of their relationship. The conversation eventually ended with an agreement to disagree for the time being. After, Joe drove Sarah home in silence.

On the way back to Baker Street, he felt so in despair that he almost didn't want to go home. Both women in his life were angry with him, and he didn't know how to fix either problem.

Right now, as he stared out at the fog settling around the automobile, he needed figure out how to deal with Irene.

Joe sighed.

Perhaps the best way was not at all. At least not right now.

It was late, but maybe he'd ring Lestrade and ask if he could stay on his couch tonight. That would solve tomorrow's breakfast dilemma – at least until Joe could figure out how to approach Irene.

Anger slithered through him, and he realized he was still mad at her. That didn't happen often. He felt frustrated, irritated and exasperated, yes. But she seemed to have a knack for smoothing things over before things reached the point of genuine anger. Tonight, however, he didn't want to see or speak to her.

As he climbed out of the Vauxhall, Joe decided that even if Lestrade didn't pick up the telephone, he'd pack a small bag and show up at his flat anyway. If that didn't work, he'd find somewhere else – anything to avoid 221B.

Joe entered the building, locking the door behind him. The

front hall was lit up, as well as the lights down toward Miss Hudson's flat. Odd. Even if the housekeeper did stay up to greet him for some reason, all the lights in the building wouldn't be on.

Perhaps she was too busy dealing with Irene or had gone to bed before either of them arrived home, and his flatmate had left all the lights on.

Joe shook his head. He was overthinking the situation to avoid going upstairs.

He wiped his boots again on the rug and trudged to the bottom of the steps. As he approached, a dark red smear on the wall caught his attention.

A succession of bloody handprints decorated the wallpaper, and his heart leapt into his throat. The third step from the bottom was covered in drying blood droplets, and heavy boot prints ran up and down the stairs, the wood still damp. Joe's stomach bottomed out. Panic swept over him, making him dizzy.

From down the hall, a door opened, and light footsteps sounded. He could have sworn he heard a bucket of water slosh. Stepping around the stairs, he prepared to meet whoever roamed the halls of his building before coming face to face with Miss Hudson.

"Joe!" she cried in surprise.

"Where's Irene?" he asked, his voice sharp and full of worry. "Is this her blood? Whose footprints are these—"

"Take a breath, love," the old woman chided, setting the bucket of water on the ground. "Irene is alright. She just had an altercation with some unfriendly men—"

"Unfriendly men?" Another surge of panic swept through him.

"All they wanted was for her to stop this investigation you both are working on. She held her own but looks the worse for it."

Joe leaned on the banister, his head still spinning. "This is my fault."

"None of that," Miss Hudson huffed. "They would've done you both in had you been with her."

He stumbled over his words as he looked at the blood again, then at the bucket of water on the floor. "Let me help you."

"Not a chance. You've both had quite the night. Get upstairs. I'll be up in ten minutes with a cuppa for you."

Joe didn't move. He wanted desperately to rush upstairs and see Irene, but his nerves and apprehension got the better of him.

"Go on, now," Miss Hudson encouraged. "She'll probably

187

be sleeping, but you can look in on her. I will warn you, Doctor, she will be just fine, but she does look quite a sight."

He headed up the stairs, every step echoing in his mind. The sitting room was eerily still and dark, forcing him to turn on the small lamp by the door. Irene's bedroom door was pulled closed but not shut tightly.

Joe slowly opened the door, letting a sliver of light from the sitting area softly illuminate her figure. She was asleep, chest rising and falling in a steady rhythm. He took a few steps into the room to get a better look at her, tiptoeing around the pile of clothes and books on the floor.

There was a large bandage over her temple. Even in the pale light, he saw dark bruises and scrapes down the side of her face. Her hand rested on the blanket, her knuckles cut up, bandages wrapping around two of them.

Joe turned away from her, looking back out into the sitting room, fighting the panic that gripped his chest. His ribs squeezed tight and he struggled to breathe. He looked around the flat, trying to calm himself. He stared at the tree, the angel hair glistening, at his pile of books, but nothing worked.

He shouldn't have let Irene walk home alone. He should've chased after her, talked her into getting back into the car. He should've tried harder to resolve their issues, but he'd let his pride get in the way. He'd hurried back to Sarah and, in turn, got Irene hurt.

A stupid argument had turned into something dangerous. His stomach churned thinking about their words.

"Joe?"

Irene's voice drifted softly through the air.

Joe realized he still held her door open, his fingers gripping the door frame. He felt dizzy and panicked, so he turned around slowly.

She propped herself up on her elbow and stared at him.

"Hi," was all he could manage, and the word came out squeaky.

Irene stared at him for a moment, then attempted to sit up. She looked at the small lamp on her bedside table, presumably to shed some light into the room. Joe put all thoughts aside and rushed forward to assist her. He turned on the lamp as Irene struggled in the bed.

"You don't need to get up. I didn't mean to disturb you. I'm sorry."

He stood awkwardly beside her bed, unsure of how to help her as she slowly sat up.

She actually laughed, then looked up at him. "Do not apologize."

Joe's breath caught in his throat as the full impact of her injuries came to light. Her eye was swollen shut, and her skin was decorated in purples and blues. His fists clenched as a sudden rush of anger washed over him. He knew Irene wasn't invincible, but he never thought he would see his friend in such a state. A part of him wanted to close his eyes tight and hope it was all a bad dream, and when he woke up, she'd be on the couch in her mismatched pyjamas right as rain.

But she was not alright. She was hurt and could barely sit up without expending all of her energy.

Irene winced, shifting in the bed, tucking herself against the wall. "Sit down. I cannot see you."

Even though her voice was weak and tired, she still gave commands as if she stood in front of a platoon of soldiers. Joe sat on the edge of the bed, shoulder to shoulder with her, one leg propped up and the other on the ground supporting him. They were both silent for a moment, then Irene wiggled on the bed. She snuggled up beside him, her head on his shoulder, arms wrapped around his bicep.

Joe thought about the conversation regarding boundaries he

had to set, but as he looked down at her with the soft light hitting her bruises and bandages, eyelashes fluttering as she peered into the sitting room, he let it go. Nothing was threatening about her at this moment.

Tears welled in his eyes. It felt like all their arguments over the past month had been futile, interfering with their friendship in the most pointless way.

Joe let his head fall back against the side of the bookcase beside the bed.

"I don't know what to say."

Irene didn't answer him. Perhaps she didn't know what to do either. He looked down at her again, but she was sleeping peacefully, curled up next to him.

He frowned as his arm was still entwined in hers. Perhaps he'd give her a few moments to fall into a deep sleep, then he'd attempt to extricate himself from her grasp.

*   *   *   *   *

Joe sat straight, a twinge in his neck, shooting pains down his shoulders and back. He was still on Irene's bed, with her fast asleep next to him. She'd released his arm and slid lower onto

191

her pillow. He immediately stood, cheeks growing hot in embarrassment. Had he spent the whole night in here? He could just make out the black hands on the light clockface: half past six in the morning.

He *had* spent the whole night in her bedroom.

He hurried to her door, then paused and headed back to her bed. The bruising looked worse today, colour settling throughout the one half of her face. He moved a bit of hair from her eyes, before tugging the blankets up to her chin. Sighing, he turned away from her, still angry with himself for leaving her alone.

Joe shut the door behind him. His whole body was stiff from falling asleep sitting up. He stretched on the way to his own room to change his clothes and wash up.

The talk he'd had with Sarah resurfaced as he climbed the stairs to his room. Guilt filled his stomach in place of breakfast. Falling asleep in Irene's bed, no matter how innocent, was definitely not respecting boundaries of any kind.

Joe's cheeks warmed again. It was as if Irene had the power to remove all trace of nerves from him and make him feel comfortable enough to act any way she welcomed.

He shook his head and headed into his small lavatory. These thoughts were simply too much before the first cup of tea.

192

*   *   *   *   *

An hour later, Joe sat at the dining table as Miss Hudson brought in breakfast. She set the tray down as Irene's bedroom door opened. The woman in question emerged, wrapped in a robe, shuffling toward the table, her eyes focused on the eggs and toast.

The landlady immediately ran to her. "Love, I was going to bring you breakfast in bed."

Irene shook her head. "I am fine, Miss Hudson. It feels good to get up."

"Are you sure you're well enough to sit out here? I could help you to the sofa." Joe set out her plate.

She shook her head and gave him a soft smile, her eyes crinkling beneath the bruises as she sat at the table. She tentatively scooped food into her mouth as Miss Hudson counted out two types of medication for her to take.

In the full light of the sitting room, Irene looked simply horrible. One side of her face was coloured in dark purples and blues. Her lip was scabbed and swollen. The bandage on her temple needed changing. Joe would check the stitches under

193

them to assure they were done to his medical standards.

Miss Hudson set the medication on the table beside her and put her hands on her hips, addressing both of them.

"Neither one of you is going anywhere today. And you are certainly not working on this case. You both need a day to relax and not think about anything and reconnect with one another."

Irene laughed. The sound came out slow and tired. "If I do not think, Miss Hudson, then I will go mad."

"You are doing *nothing*, young lady," the old woman scolded, then gave a final nod of her head before leaving the room.

Joe frowned at Irene. She may be able to think, but not much else. Her whole body seemed exhausted.

He still felt a bit of guilt in his stomach. The feeling must have shown on his face because she groaned.

"Don't, Joe. It's not your fault. This happened because we are close to solving this case. If you were there, they would've done much worse to you, I'm sure."

She was correct, but that didn't ease the guilt he felt. "Irene, I am truly sorry—"

"I do not want to discuss it."

"I think we should, though."

194

"Oh, we will," she said. Joe caught a smirk on her lips. "Once I am well enough."

He accepted this answer and watched her struggle to eat for a moment before eventually turning away to focus on his own meal.

"You know what this means, though?" she asked. "We *are* close to solving this. We've hit upon a large piece of the puzzle, Joe. Between this attack and the automobile trying to run me off the road the other night, we—"

Joe jerked his head up, completely blindsided by her statement. "What automobile?"

Irene appeared panicked for a moment, then waved him off. "Someone was tailing me on the way home from Jeannie's. I lost them. Not a big deal."

"Why didn't you tell me?"

"Because the worry on your face would have annoyed me to no end." She kept her voice nonchalant as she finished her meal.

All Joe could do was stare at her. She was right, he would've worried, and he definitely wouldn't have let her walk away by herself last night.

He thumped his fork on the dining table like a judge banging a gavel.

"From this moment on, we let the professionals handle it. We did our job and passed on the information. Now we let Cullens and Digby do what they do best."

Irene looked like she wanted to argue but kept at her toast instead. Joe had a feeling that she had a plan up her sleeve, or perhaps she simply didn't have the energy to argue with him.

"What did Lestrade say when you told him about last night?" he asked.

Irene shrugged.

"He doesn't know?"

"He will only fret and try to track down who did this. And he doesn't need to be in any danger. Please do not tell him – at least not until the case is over and I am healing."

It was Joe's turn to swallow an argument. He sighed, knowing that this day would be filled with lots of tiptoeing around specific issues until they were both in the right mindset.

*   *   *   *   *

Thankfully, the day went by as calm as ever.

Irene drifted in and out of sleep on the sofa, while Joe attempted to keep from staring at her wounds.

The doctor came in to check on her after lunch, and Joe stood by the entire time. The stitches were nicely done, putting his mind at ease. Once the examination finished, Irene retired to bed in the early evening.

Joe thought about calling Sarah but decided to give it one more day. He wanted to see her, but he wasn't too keen on having any sort of in-depth conversation with her. Not right now.

After a late supper by himself, Joe went to bed as well and felt pretty good about what tomorrow would bring.

*   *   *   *   *

The next morning, he found Irene in the sitting room, looking much perkier than the day before. She stared at the board while munching on toast. She still chewed gingerly but seemed to have some determination behind her.

"I am still trying to connect Bernadette and Mr. Barnes."

Joe wandered over to her, a cup of tea in his hand. "I thought we weren't talking about the case."

"That was yesterday. But today, we need to get a move on."

He wanted to argue, but realized that if all she did was sit here and run ideas past him, there would surely be no harm.

197

"If Timothy dies," Irene continued, "then Bernadette has the business. Mr. Barnes *wants* the business, so does she *give* him the business?"

"How do we know they've ever spoken? It seems to me that Bernadette and Timothy stay away from the store."

She tapped her roughened finger to her lips in thought. "Perhaps she didn't need to speak to him at all. AB could have organized everything so that speaking to one another wasn't necessary. All Bernadette would need to do is sign the business over."

Joe stared at the board, struggling to put the connection together. "What does she have to gain from a dead husband and no business?"

"Perhaps it's not to gain anything," Irene mused. "If AB killed Bernadette's husband, then perhaps it is some form of a traded favour."

"Or payment." He still couldn't quite see the connection or reasoning behind the theory, but he felt the gears in his own head turn. Even though he said he was done with the case, he still felt the need to work out the clues. It frustrated him to no end, making him feel hypocritical for scolding Irene for doing the same thing.

Suddenly, she gripped his forearm and gave a small gasp as whatever realization swept over her. "Joe, you are brilliant."

"Am I? I don't see how, in this instance."

Irene grabbed a piece of chalk and drew lines and arrows across the board. "Bernadette doesn't come from much money at all. What if she needed her husband killed but couldn't afford it? She would owe AB a favour or two. Perhaps this is the woman now turning in the favour. What if Mr. Barnes went to AB to remove Timothy from the equation, but the first attempt went awry? Then, Barnes finds out he isn't even in Timothy's will to begin with, and AB has to find another way to get the business to Barnes. She is clever; she would've figured out this was the best way to get each party what they wanted."

Joe nodded, seeing where her reasoning was going. "So, she forces Bernadette into a marriage, to then kill Timothy so she can give the business to Mr. Barnes. Everyone wins."

"Except Timothy."

He stared at his partner for a moment and felt a jolt of excitement. Had they really solved this case?

Irene buzzed with the same excitement. "This is brilliant. This is exactly what I would do had I been presented with this problem."

"Irene!" Joe playfully scolded. "Let's hope you *never* get this opportunity."

She started towards the door, shifting slowly step by step.

"Where are you going?" He caught up to her, his arms out in case she toppled over.

"To confront Bernadette."

All the playfulness left Joe's voice, quickly replaced with frustration and exasperation. "Irene, you are in no shape to do *anything*. You shouldn't even be out of bed."

"I'm fine." She cried out in pain as she bent for her boots, collapsing against the wall.

Joe rushed forward. "You are *not*."

He scooped her up to carry her to her bed, but she wiggled out of his grasp and fell to the ground.

"Goodness' sake, Irene. Why must you be so damn stubborn?"

He extended his hand to help her up, but she slapped it away.

"I'm *fine* and seeing this case through. I am confronting Bernadette myself and saving Timothy from being murdered."

"*You* will be the one who ends up dead if you walk out of here," he argued, then gestured to her hunched over figure

200

taking aid from the back of the sofa. "You can't even walk. Your wounds are too great for—"

"Oh, what do you know?" she snapped at him, wincing again as she attempted to straighten.

"I'm a doctor." he retorted hotly.

"Of animals." She finally stood straight, tears in her eyes, jaw clenched in pain. "I'm not some horse you can whisper to and tame."

"I'm not trying to tame you," he said, the words tasting foul in his mouth. "I'm trying to get you to use common sense."

Irene attempted to hide the pain she was in as she moved to the door, but Joe caught how she limped and hunched her shoulder as she cradled her arm. His face reddened and he was tempted to just let her go and watch how far she got before collapsing.

He stood still for a moment, trying to ease the anger and frustration inside, his stomach turning, ribs tightening over his lungs.

Then, he rushed to the door, cutting in front of Irene and blocking her exit.

She looked up at him with the same dark raging eyes as the night before, and he swore they peered into his soul.

"Move, Joe."

"No." He held his arms out to further his stance against her.

"I'll make you move," she warned. The threat almost made him step aside, but he stood firm.

"Not in your condition, you won't. Sit down, and I will—"

She grabbed his arm and pulled. He resisted, using his height against her. He raised his arm, forcing her hands up.

Irene cried out in pain and recoiled, a hand clutching her injured shoulder. She looked at him then with the most hateful glare he'd ever seen, tears welling in her eyes.

He immediately felt guilty, but then anger worked its way in there, and he squared his shoulders. They stared at each other for a moment in a stand-off of pure will.

After a few seconds, though, Irene's eyes fluttered, and she swayed on the spot before her knees buckled. All of Joe's anger and frustration were swept aside as he rushed forward to help her. He caught her before she collapsed to the ground, bringing her to her feet.

"Leave me alone," she mumbled, shrugging him off.

She shuffled to her bedroom, slamming the door behind her.

Joe let her go. He leaned on the couch, taking deep breaths, willing his ribs to release his lungs. He was weary from their battles. They were doing so well today, solving the case like their old selves.

He sat on the arm of the sofa and sighed, at a loss for what to do. Perhaps it would be better if he found somewhere else to stay – or even somewhere else to live – just until their friendship mended. If it ever did. He couldn't quite see how they could come back from their recent arguments, especially once he started putting more boundaries in place.

How those boundaries would affect their cases together, he had no idea. A part of him wasn't sure he even wanted to put limits in place at all. He was never bothered by his and Irene's closeness. It was comforting to have someone walk arm in arm with him, kiss him on the head, hug him when something exciting happened.

Perhaps that was Sarah's point. *She* was supposed to do all that. But she wasn't here for exciting things. There were no joyous celebrations of a solved mystery or long strolls down the pavement to venues that held answers to cases.

Joe groaned and rubbed his forehead. These intrusive thoughts were not something he wanted to deal with right now.

Irene was injured and needed a good couple of weeks to heal. This case had to go away before it ruined anything else in their lives. *Then* Joe would deal with his friendship with Irene and his relationship with Sarah.

He glanced at his partner's bedroom, but no noise came from beyond the closed door.

* * * * *

Joe didn't know how long he sat on the sofa staring at the board, procrastinating everything he needed to do, but eventually, he stood and looked at the clock.

Early afternoon.

He'd decided to ring Mr. Cullens to give him their new findings and inform him that they were done.

He felt a little guilty going behind Irene's back, but this case had torn so much of their lives apart. What was one more thing for her to mad at him about?

As the call connected, he fiddled with the notepad they kept by the telephone, stealing one more glance at the bedroom door.

"Digby speaking."

"Oh, hello, Mr. Digby. I was expecting Mr. Cullens. My apologies."

"Not to worry, young man. He's stepped out for the moment. This is Doctor Watson, correct?"

204

"Yes, sir," Joe said, slightly surprised that the man had remembered his name. "I know we have been a bit back and forth about the continued investigation, but we are finished with it now, I assure you."

"Jolly good!" Digby said, a little too enthusiastically for Joe's liking.

"We do have one last bit of information to pass on, if you're still willing to accept it. In fact, it may be the clue that solves every one of these smaller cases as well."

Digby hesitated, seemingly in shock. "Well, I would very much be interested in the information you've acquired. How about we meet and have a little chat?"

Joe looked at Irene's door. "I'm not sure I can meet. It's crucial information, I realize, but I don't think—"

"Dear boy. Do you think you've completely solved this case?"

"Yes."

"And have you confronted the parties involved?"

"Not yet, as we were going to let you do it. Though Irene is quite keen – and she will seek them out, I'm sure, the first chance she gets. Which is why I wanted to call, so you can finish the case quickly."

"And we most certainly will. I'd like to bring Cullens into this as well if I can track him down. Why don't you meet us at the Dozen Pips pub in Holloway immediately? We can grab a late bite to eat and you can give us the information."

Joe's stomach stirred at agreeing to the meet without Irene's knowledge, but the image of her bruised and battered face flashed in his mind, giving him the confidence that this was the correct choice.

"Excellent," he said to Digby, scribbling the pub's name on the pad. "See you shortly."

He set the receiver down and heard Miss Hudson arrive home. He made his way downstairs and caught up to her just as she reached the door to her own flat.

"Miss Hudson."

The woman turned and smiled presently at him. "How's our wee lass doing?"

"She's stubborn. We just had a particularity nasty row."

"Oh, dear!"

"I have to step out," he said before the landlady could ask more. "I'm passing the rest of this case off to Cullens and Digby."

"That's for the best. I will look after her."

"She's in a mood. Admittedly, I'm responsible for it."

Miss Hudson waved him off. "Never you mind. Off you go."

Joe hurried back up the stairs and threw on his jacket, hat and shoes. He didn't know the Holloway district of London very well, so he'd leave early. He grabbed the piece of paper with the pub's name from the table, hastily shoving it into the pocket.

Truthfully, he needed to leave before Irene emerged because he didn't want to go through another argument. She would demand to come with him, which simply wasn't possible.

He glanced at her doorway one last time for good measure, then headed out.

*   *   *   *   *

After the fifteen minutes it took to get to Holloway, it took Joe another ten to find Dozen Pips pub. He'd driven past it several times as well, simply because in his rush, the piece of paper he thought he put in his pocket had somehow fallen out back at Baker Street.

The road was calm and Joe found a spot right in front of the building. He parked behind another black automobile, which he assumed belonged to Digby or Cullens. Hardly any pedestrians walked the street which made for an eery, yet somewhat pleasant scene.

The pub appeared closed. All the lights were off. Utterly confused, Joe started back to the car.

"Doctor Watson!" Mr. Digby's voice came from a small alleyway beside the building. Joe walked around and found the man standing by the pub's side door. He gave a little wave. It was odd to find him alone, but perhaps this was part of the plan when government workers met to discuss investigations.

"The pub looks closed," Joe said as he approached. "Should we try somewhere else? Also, were you able to reach Mr. Cullens?"

Digby sighed as if disappointed.

"I am sorry, Doctor," he said, reaching into his jacket. He pulled out a small pistol and pointed the barrel straight at Joe.

"What's going on?"

"I need you to do exactly as I say," Digby said. "And I won't have to harm you at all."

"Harm me? Mr. Cullens—"

"Forget about Cullens. He isn't here. Turn around slowly. We're going to my automobile."

Joe stood for a moment, frozen, eyes glued to the gun. He needed to escape, but he had absolutely no idea how.

What would Irene do?

He swept his eyes over Digby, attempting to deduce something, *anything*. A twig was stuck to the man's arm, and he had a particular-looking kind of mud stuck to his shoe, even though the ground around here was dry.

Digby, clearly unhappy with Joe's hesitation, shoved his shoulder.

Slowly, Joe turned, attempting to breathe in the cold air, his ribs threatening to pop his lungs into bits. "Does Cullens even know you're here?"

"Of course not."

They reached the end of the alley. Digby tugged on Joe's arm, steering him towards the black car parked in front of the Vauxhall. Mud was splotched on the tires. As they approached, he knew he needed to get it off. He feigned a trip and stumbled into the car, kicking a chunk of mud off with his shoe.

Digby growled a curse word and yanked him off the car.

Joe stepped back, pretending to stumble backwards this time. He stepped on the man's shoe, hoping to leave enough of a footprint on the pavement.

"Get off of me! Don't make this difficult, Doctor. Get in the car."

Joe still needed to get the twig from Digby's jacket, but he had no idea how. Unless...

The idea was stupid and dangerous and might get him shot, but his instinct told him to leave as many clues possible.

He grabbed Digby's arm as if to wrestle the gun from him.

Digby reacted, grabbing Joe's wrist and twisting. The twig fell to the ground, and Joe submitted immediately.

Digby laughed. "Nice try, Doctor. Get in the car."

Joe opened the door and slid into the back seat, his wrist throbbing.

Digby threw a pair of handcuffs at him, then grabbed a burlap sack from the floor, tossing it at Joe as well.

"Put both of those on."

Joe secured the handcuffs around his wrists, keeping them relatively loose.

"Tighter," Digby ordered.

He reluctantly obeyed, squeezing the metal until it touched his entire wrist. He picked up the bag, then hesitated, feeling oddly bold.

"What if I don't? Are you really going to shoot me?"

Digby leaned into the car and pressed the cool muzzle of the gun to his temple. "You want to find out?"

210

Joe felt his blood run cold. He knew he could push the bluff, but didn't want to. As he put the bag over his head, he cursed himself for feeling so useless and weak. Irene had just taken on three men in an alley a few nights ago, and here he was letting an elderly gentlemen push him into a car.

Digby tightened the bag, securing it before slamming the door. Joe heard the driver's door open and shut, then the man started the engine. Within seconds, they drove out into the streets of London.

Chapter XI

A Rescue Mission

Irene paused at her bedroom door, listening for any noises from the sitting room. While she was never one to back down from a confrontation, she didn't want to cross Joe if she didn't have to. That's if he even wanted to speak to her again. She was two for two, inciting a fight when it wasn't necessary. He would probably only take so much before he left the flat, either for a break or permanently.

She groaned as her stomach flipped, leaving her nauseous. She didn't want to think about Joe leaving. As frustrated as she was with him, she couldn't bear the thought of him finding another home.

Silence still filled the air, so she opened the door an inch and peered out. The sitting room was empty, so it was safe to use the lavatory.

When she was finished, Irene wandered out and stood in the empty sitting room. Joe's hat was gone from its hook. The fire had dwindled. He'd gone out somewhere – probably over to Sarah's.

A piece of paper sat on the floor by the telephone table. She scooped it up, wincing as a dull pain throbbed in her shoulder.

Joe's writing scribbled hastily, reading:

Dozen Pips Pub - Holloway

Irene stared at the writing for a moment before setting the paper next to the telephone. Where was he going?

She shook her head. It didn't matter. He'd made it perfectly clear that he was done with the case – that *they* were done. He was probably meeting Sarah or Michael.

Those thoughts started up a whole new line of feelings that sucker-punched her in the gut. She'd been so hurtful toward Joe for having friends just because she never made an effort to have any of her own.

She stared at the empty flat. Hopefully Miss Hudson heard her up and about and was bringing tea. She needed a good cuppa right about now.

The telephone rang, the noise echoing in the quiet room. Irene startled. It rang again and she winced, the sharp tone

213

cutting through her still fuzzy head.

"Irene Holmes speaking," she picked up, leaning on the small table.

"You are *persistent*, Miss Holmes."

She instantly recognized the woman's voice. AB had dropped all hints of her fake English accent and let the touch of German flow through her words.

Irene gripped the receiver tight, her heart thudding in her ears, but she couldn't help the small grin that came over her face.

"I'll take that as a compliment."

AB laughed on the other end of the phone. "I gave you ample opportunities to back out of this investigation, and yet you refused. Not even my associates threatening you in that alley could sway you."

"Clearly, you need better negotiators," Irene said. "You will not win. I have everything figured out. All the deals you orchestrated, all the people you hired, all the mistakes you made."

The woman laughed again, but the sound was tinged with annoyance. "It is *you* who has now made a mistake. You sent your little pet out to finish your job. The good doctor isn't as tough as you or as clever."

Irene's blood grew cold, freezing her for a moment. Her breath caught in her throat, and a tremor snaked through her hand.

Joe.

"What did you do to him?" Her words came out icy as she stared at the phone, willing her anger to travel though the lines right to AB.

"Nothing…yet. And I don't want to do anything to him. Walk away from the case, Miss Holmes, and you shall have your doctor back unharmed."

"The case is done," Irene snapped.

"That solution you think you have? You will keep it to yourself, and you will telephone Mr. Cullens and tell him that you don't believe the cases are linked at all, now that you've thought about it."

"That's not—"

"You're not understanding, Miss Holmes. If you—"

"*You* do not understand *me*," Irene stood straight, anger fuelling her words. "I will get Joe back *and* see you behind bars."

"I admire the tenacity. But if you pursue this case, then the only way you will get your doctor back is piece by piece in the post. Drop the case. Once I have confirmation you've done what I've asked, then I will let him go. Goodbye, Miss Holmes."

The line went dead, the tone buzzing in Irene's ear. She stood frozen for a moment, still clutching the receiver, consumed with thoughts about Joe. How was he taken? *Who* had taken him? Was he hurt?

A jolt of anger hit her, and she slammed the receiver down. "Shit!"

"Irene Holmes!" The door flew open, Miss Hudson entering with tea tray in her hands. "You will *not* use that kind of language in here—"

"She took him," Irene whirled around to the older woman. "She has Joe. I must get him back."

The landlady quickly set the tea tray down and rushed back to her, clutching her wrists.

"You're shaking, love. Tell me what happened."

Irene hadn't realized she had tremors running through her arms and hands. She shook with adrenaline and anger and determination.

"The men who attacked me work for someone who wants us to drop this case," she said as calmly as she could, but her words came out urgent and choppy. "And we— *I* didn't listen, and now she's got Joe. I have to get him back."

Miss Hudson gave her wrists a gentle tug, snapping her back to the room.

"You are going nowhere in your condition."

"My condition doesn't matter—"

"It does," Miss Hudson snapped. "You won't save Joe like this. You will only hurt yourself more and might put him in greater danger."

Irene refused to listen. Instead, she pressed her for more information.

"Did Joe say anything to you before he left?"

The woman sighed but gave Irene the information anyway: "He said he was going to meet Cullens and Digby to give them the rest of the information about the case. That was it."

Irene took her hands back and pressed her finger to her lips in thought. She stared at the board for a moment, then spun to the housekeeper.

"I need to think," she said. "Leave."

Miss Hudson folded her arms across her chest. "Irene Holmes, do not speak to me like—"

"I'm sorry, alright?" she cried, panic filling her voice. "I'm

217

sorry. Just please be silent for a moment so I can stop my damn head from spinning and figure out what to do."

But the woman didn't let up. "What you can do is call Eddy and—"

"Miss Hudson, please!" Irene clasped her hands together, begging the woman to listen. She hated disturbances on the best of days, but with her energy limited and her head still cloudy, she needed all the concentration and focus she could muster.

Miss Hudson held her hands up in surrender but kept the scowl on her face.

Irene knew that if she called Eddy, she'd never see Joe again. As soon as AB got wind of police presence anywhere near her, she'd kill him and flee.

Irene couldn't take that chance. But she also couldn't walk out of here alone without the persistent lady dragging her back in and sealing the flat shut.

Guilt worked its way in with the worry swirling in Irene's gut, and she looked at Miss Hudson.

"I will call Eddy. I just need a moment to gather my thoughts."

Miss Hudson narrowed her eyes like she didn't quite believe Irene's words, but eventually, she nodded.

"Good. We will get Joe back, don't you worry. Eddy will have the whole of Scotland Yard out looking for him. You know that."

Irene nodded and glanced at the two bottles of pills on the tea tray, then at the sandwich, a plan forming in her mind.

She just needed Miss Hudson to leave, but the woman hesitated, then sighed.

"Your Uncle John was once held hostage after doing something foolish for your father. Sherlock never admitted it, but he felt guilty for weeks afterwards."

"I remember Uncle John telling me about it." Irene pulled the story from her memory. "I guess Father and I have a knack for putting people we love in danger."

She didn't mean for the words to come out as bitter as they sounded, but the more she allowed her brain to process the situation, the more she realized that some of the anger was directed toward herself for allowing Joe to be taken.

Suddenly, she didn't know if she referred to his kidnapping or their lives in general, which stirred up a whole other pool of feelings.

Miss Hudson must have taken her silence as contemplation because she touched her bruised cheek. "Call Eddy, then eat and

219

take your medication."

When the old woman left the room, Irene listened for a moment, making sure she started down the stairs to the first floor.

As soon as the steps creaked, Irene turned towards the dining table. Squaring her shoulders, she felt determination creep in, and she let it consume her.

She took a big bite of the sandwich and grabbed the bottle of pills. She poured half a dozen caplets into her hand, then tossed them into her mouth. By the time she made it to wherever Joe was taken, the medication would activate and help her last long enough to free him.

As soon as she was done with her food, she put on trousers and a sweater, and grabbed Uncle John's revolver from her bedside table, hastily loading bullets into the cylinder. Hopefully it didn't come down to the gun, but Irene didn't want to walk into AB's lair unarmed either.

Next was the small chemistry table beside the lavatory. She yanked open the middle drawer and rooted around half a dozen small pouches. She snatched the dark blue one that belonged to Uncle John. She dumped out the contents onto the table, and five small glass tubes of smelling salts wrapped in cotton rolled onto the table. She cracked one, holding it to her nose. The ammonia jolted her to life and she coughed as the fumes worked their way into her body.

She stuck two more tubes of the smelling salts into her pocket.

Irene was determined to get Joe back, even if it killed her.

In her condition, it just might.

*   *   *   *   *

Sneaking out of 221B was surprisingly easy. Soon Irene sat in the back of a taxicab, riding through the streets of London on her way to Dozen Pips pub. The driver kept glancing back at her, wary of her bruises and urgent manner. Her eyes felt huge as well, no doubt the result of the smelling salts.

The adrenaline and anger still coursed through her and, mixed with the guilt and worry, made her dizzy. She was worried about Joe, of course, and the pain she felt in her chest reminded her that his place in her life went beyond colleague and even beyond friend. He was her family, having secured a place in her heart next to her father, Uncle John, Miss Hudson and Eddy.

And it was her fault that he was captured. If she'd listened to him about the investigation – or about the many other things he'd said throughout it – then perhaps they'd both be safe at Baker Street right now. If she'd communicated her emotions in the past few months as much as he shared his own, maybe they wouldn't have been arguing as much just mere weeks before Christmas.

Instead, she was in the back of a taxicab on her way to rescue her best friend while high on smelling salts because of a fight that she shouldn't have been involved in anyway.

Irene shook her head, her leg bouncing up and down. Her body was ready to do something with all the false energy from the medication.

She could think of what she should have done for ages and never feel any better. Right now, she needed to concentrate and hope that something at the Dozen Pips gave her a clue as to where Joe was.

As soon as the taxi got within half a block of the pub, Irene spotted the Vauxhall and her heart leapt into her throat. The cab pulled up behind it, and she paid her fare. The driver gave her another curious look before speeding away.

She tugged her coat tighter, the cool air giving her a chill as her boots thumped down the pavement toward the pub.

The street was quiet, with most of the buildings still in various states of repair, the effects from the buzz bombs that scarred the area. The Dozen Pips appeared closed, either for good or until evening.

Irene immediately went to her car, searching for any clues. When it came up empty-handed, she slammed the door in frustration. The automobile appeared unscathed, which meant Joe had exited the car. Whether by force or with his own will, Irene had yet to determine.

She tried to look for footprints, but the ground was dry. She crouched, ignoring the dull pain in her shoulder and stomach. A small twig was caught in a crack in the pavement. Irene picked it up: a piece of tall, dry grass, one that wouldn't be found in the middle of London.

Curious.

Near it, very faint and drying, was a footprint. Irene pressed herself practically flat, studying it. She fished her small magnifying glass from her pocket and ran it over the mark. A pattern in the middle of captured her attention.

Mr. Digby's shoe.

She recognized the unique pattern from the wet mat he stood

on when he visited 221B earlier in the week.

Fuelled by a fit of new anger, she kept up her search, hunching over and scouring the ground. In front of the Vauxhall were traces of another automobile. A few chunks of mud and dirt were smeared on the curb as if they'd fallen off a tire. She scooped some into her hand, squishing it between her fingers, discovering that was coated in some sort of slime.

Out of habit, she turned to where Joe usually stood at her shoulder, but frowned at the empty space.

There was a faint outline of a shoe print in the smeared mud. She measured it with her hand and looked through her magnifying glass. A grin broke out over her face as tears sprung to her eyes for a reason she didn't understand.

Joe's shoeprint! It was as if he'd purposefully stepped in the muck or kicked it off the tire himself.

"Clever man."

Irene sat on the curb for a moment, adrenaline still coursing through her. A proud smile formed on her lips as she thought of him leaving clues for her to find. Perhaps she'd rubbed off on him a bit. The feeling didn't ease her worry but fuelled her determination to find her friend.

But where had Digby taken him? Dry grasses, moist, sticky

mud, obviously somewhere seclusive. She pulled a map of London into her mind and tried to pinpoint where he could be. It couldn't be too far away because AB had rung Irene within an hour or so of Joe leaving Baker Street.

The roar of a police siren interrupted her thoughts as three vehicles rushed down the street towards her.

She'd expected Miss Hudson to find her missing, but she hadn't expected her to have phoned Eddy so quickly. His Wolseley police car charged down the road toward her.

The automobile screeched to a stop beside the curb in front of her. The inspector's eyes widened as he took in her appearance, bruises and all.

"What the *hell* happened? Miss Hudson said you were attacked. Who did this? What is going on!?"

"Eddy," Irene said, keeping her voice as calm as she could. "I need to find Joe."

The detective walked in a circle, attempting to calm himself. The two other police cars stopped. As soon as the constables were out of the vehicles, Eddy barked at them.

"Secure the street! Both ends."

They jumped into action. He whirled back to Irene.

"If you were in this much danger, why wouldn't you ring

me? Tell me what is going on *now.*"

"The case we're working on has become a bit hairy."

"A bit hairy?" Lestrade snapped, his voice cracking in frustration. "Have you seen your face? Have you seen where we are? You look like the piss has been knocked out of you."

Irene sighed. "Okay, so a bit hairy is an understatement. Things are not good, Eddy. But I am in the process of fixing everything. I simply need—"

He held up his finger to silence her, his eyes running over her broken appearance once more.

"The last time I spoke to either one of you, you were on your way to chat with a former soldier, and neither one had a scratch upon you. That was only *three* days ago!"

He took a moment to compose himself while Irene waited. She was anxious to leave this scene and contemplate her findings. It came as no surprise that Miss Hudson had called Eddy, but she was rather annoyed that she now had to escape him *and* four constables. She felt a bit woozy and knew she needed another whiff of those smelling salts. The medicine was finally dulling her shoulder pain, but they didn't help much with her exhaustion. Her fingers were tingling, but that was probably just an unfortunate side effect of too many pills.

226

"We were told to stop investigating," Irene explained, "but we didn't listen. You remember Mr. Digby?"

"The older man who came to claim the files? I remember him."

"He's the one that took Joe. I found his footprint and Miss Hudson confirmed it earlier. Joe was meeting him here. I assume he works for the woman orchestrating this whole mess."

Saying those words out loud caused the ball of anger in Irene's stomach to grow. She needed to find Joe before it turned into something she couldn't control.

Eddy blew out a breath and glanced around the street.

"Let me consult my men, and we'll start a search. Meanwhile, go sit in my automobile until we're done, and I can drive you back home."

Irene trudged to the Wolseley and climbed in the passenger side. The keys were still in the ignition. A mischievous thought crossed her mind, but movement came from her peripherals and dashed any wandering ideas.

A constable knocked on the window and smiled when Irene rolled it down.

"Inspector Lestrade wants the window down in case he has questions for you."

Irene obliged, slumping in the seat, battling the tiredness about to sweep over her.

Where could Digby have taken Joe? She went over the clues in her mind, compiling theories. Dry grasses and gooey mud in a spot somewhere reasonably close. She clamped her eyes shut, running through London in her mind. Where would it be that wet this time of year?

Her eyes popped open as the answer smacked her in the face.

"The warehouses by the wetlands," she mumbled a little louder than she meant to. "Of course."

The constable still standing next to her bent to the window. "What was that, Miss?"

She waved him off, throwing a rather annoyed look at him. "I'm just talking to myself."

That seemed to satisfy him, but he never left the automobile. Eddy must've ordered him to stand guard, lest Irene attempt some scheme.

How well he knew her.

Irene stared at the keys. Usually, Eddy took them with him, this being a police automobile after all, but he must've forgotten them in his rush. She looked through the windows and watched

228

the constables moving about, searching the grounds. She had limited time before the inspector would arrive at the car to take her home, so whatever she needed to do, she had to act quickly.

She was still sure that if she rolled up to some warehouse with a herd of Police vehicles, AB would flee, and she would never hear from her again. Or worse, she'd kill Joe, silencing the doctor from whatever he witnessed her do or say, *then* flee.

That thought made Irene sick to her stomach. She fished in her pocket for another vile of smelling salts to give herself a boost for the drive.

The constable still stood guard, so she called him over.

"Tell Inspector Lestrade that I found clues around the back of the building. Hurry up."

He hesitated, but Irene scowled.

"Do you want to be of help or not? Go!"

He took off, running right to Eddy.

Irene broke the vial of smelling salts, sucking in the fumes, breathing hard from the smell. She tossed the bundle away and took a few deep breaths, heart racing.

She clambered over to the driver's side and turned the key. As soon as the engine caught, she threw the car into gear. She didn't look back to see if anyone was following her; she simply drove down the street, speeding past the other police automobile parked at the end.

"Hang in there, Joe," she mumbled to the windshield, her right eye twitching from the medication and salts. "I'm coming to save you."

Chapter XII

A Showdown in an Abandoned Warehouse

Joe stretched his aching shoulders as best he could in the small wooden chair. heavy rope tied his body down, securing him to the back of the seat. Digby had taken his handcuffs away but made sure to tighten his new restraints so he could barely breathe. He shivered as a draft blew through the small warehouse. His jacket and gloves were still on, but sitting stagnant in an open space was not conducive to keeping warm.

"Cold, Doctor?"

Joe cringed at the female voice purring behind him. He'd seen AB from afar when Digby had shoved him into the warehouse, but this was the first time in the twenty minutes he'd been sitting here that she'd come close.

Her tall figure moved around to the front of him, her thick heels clicking on the cement floor. Her fur jacket hung down to her calves, and her blonde hair was done up in high rolls, making her appear well over six feet tall. Large rings adorned a few of her fingers; Joe couldn't help but think they were all stolen.

Her blue eyes fixed on him, never blinking or straying, seemingly waiting for his answer. He squirmed. He had no idea how to get out of this predicament, but he needed to stay calm. She hadn't killed him yet, so she must still need him.

"What are you trying to do?" he said, his voice hoarse from the cold.

She smiled down at him, like a wild cat before it pounced. "Same as everyone else. Surviving."

A young man jogged into the building and approached AB "He's returned to headquarters."

"Wonderful. As soon as I get word that Miss Holmes has dropped the case, then you are free to go."

Joe huffed a defeated laugh. "Just like that?"

"Of course. I don't need to make an enemy of Irene Holmes. The less contact I have with her, the better."

He looked up at the woman, curious as to the meaning behind her words. "You sound like you're scared of what she could do to you."

AB let out a string of light, amused laughter and patted Joe hard on the head. "Silly boy. She is like a tick that makes me itch. She cannot stop me, but she is a nuisance that I don't want to deal with. She brings unwanted attention to the intricacies of my dealings, and that police friend of hers is swift and organized whenever she calls upon him."

"Funny. Irene likened you to something similar. Now that I've met you, I'm inclined to agree."

He had no idea where his sudden confidence came from, but he hoped it paid off. Perhaps because he'd been in seemingly much worse situations, or because he assumed, like with all the other dire predicaments he and Irene got into, that this one would turn out just fine.

AB slapped him across the face. "Obviously, she hasn't taught you how to speak to a lady."

Joe's cheek stung, the cold air fuelling the pain. The anger he'd felt for the past few days crept up inside him, and he looked at AB "She will not drop the case, not even for me. *Especially* not for me."

"I beg to differ. She sounded quite worried about you when I rang her."

Joe chuckled despite himself. "If you rang her, then you've

only fuelled the fire. She'll be on her way here by now."

That seemed to irk the woman. She stood closer to Joe, towering over him.

"If she finds me, then neither one of you will make it out alive. Unless..."

She gazed down at him with that same predatory look as before. Joe avoided her eyes, staring off to the side of the warehouse instead. The fur from her jacket was mere inches from his face. He tried his best to keep the feeling contained, but AB must've noticed.

She ran her finger gently down his cheek, and when she spoke, her words were low and seductive. "How was the war for you, Doctor? Was it rough?"

"I'm not answering that," Joe snapped, trying to move his head away.

She crouched down in front of him. Her finger moved down his neck, brushing his chest, and her hand came to rest on his thigh.

Joe's cheeks grew warm, and he tried to squirm away, but the damn chair wouldn't budge.

"I have yet to acquire a skilled medical man," she said, staring up at him, voice still low. "You and I could leave here together. I could give you everything you want."

"I have everything I want," he replied stiffly, but his voice wavered, his ribs squeezing his lungs. Things were turning sour, and he had no idea how to get out of this situation.

"You do?" She leaned forward, pausing at his ear. "I don't think that's true."

She stood and counted off on her fingers. "You get dragged around by Miss Holmes to places you do not want to go, and now your love life is being interfered with."

Joe couldn't hide the surprise in his expression as he met her gaze.

She laughed. "I have eyes and ears everywhere, Doctor. Meeting your true love is hard when you have a tag-a-long as prominent as Miss Holmes. Come with me and you can have the librarian, a house, and children if you so desire. You can have everything you want, as quickly as you want it. I would only ask for your skills every now and then."

Joe stared at her. The way she spoke, so confident in her promise, stirred some part of him and forced him to keep listening.

"There really is no trick. I wouldn't make you do anything you couldn't do. I'm sure Irene has pushed you to do all sorts of uncomfortable things in the 'name of investigations', but I wouldn't be so cruel."

The mention of Irene snapped Joe back to reality. The anger he'd felt suddenly turned toward AB. How dare she make assumptions about his and Irene's friendship?

He realized, then, that this was her skill. This was how she coerced everyone to work for her. But she'd underestimated the bond that he and Irene shared. She didn't understand how deep their friendship truly ran.

Neither had Joe until this moment. He would never go against Irene. He would never flip sides or walk away from her because the grass was seemingly greener on the other side. And he certainly wouldn't leave her to become a criminal, or whatever it was AB was offering.

"Oh, dear. You look determined, Doctor." She grabbed his jaw, forcing his head up to look at her. "You would never join me, would you? At least not on your own. But I bet you'd follow along if Irene did."

"She'd never join you, either," Joe said through clenched teeth.

"You think too highly of your precious friend."

"And you underestimate her." He wrenched his head out of

her grasp.

A gunshot sounded outside the warehouse. Then another. Then two more in quick succession.

AB whirled toward the sound, giving Joe an opportunity. He kicked her leg and her knee buckled, but she didn't go down. She pivoted and backhanded him, the ring on her finger leaving a large gash in his cheek.

He cried out in pain as warm liquid oozed down his face and dripped onto the cement below his feet. He blinked back tears when the cold air stung the wound.

As his vision cleared, he heard a metal door open. When he looked to see where the noise came from, AB grabbed a chunk of his hair, forcing his head up. He struggled to get free, prickling pain coursing through his head, but the cold muzzle of a revolver against his temple stopped any more movement.

The door toward the front of the warehouse wrenched open and Irene entered, her uncle's army revolver up and ready to shoot. She spotted Joe and AB and aimed right for the woman's chest.

Joe's heart sunk right to his stomach. His partner was in no shape to be away from Baker Street, let alone here rescuing him. She stood about twenty feet away from them. From where he sat, Joe could see her shaking hand clenched at her side. Her pupils were dilated and her breathing was erratic, as if she was on a strange concoction of drugs.

However, a part of him was relieved that someone was here to rescue him, even if it was his friend who looked to be on the brink of death.

Now that the women were locked in a stand-off, AB released Joe's hair but kept the gun on him.

"My men certainly did a number on that pretty face of yours, didn't they?"

"Release him," Irene snapped, her voice gravelly and hoarse, "and I'll consider letting you walk out of here alive."

AB ignored her request. "My men out there didn't even get a shot off, did they? Did you kill them?"

"Drop the gun and find out for yourself."

Despite Irene's dreadful appearance, she appeared ready to take on the world. Her dark eyes were hooded and rimmed in bruises. Her hair was coming loose from its tie, and her black trousers and matching black coat gave her a villainous appearance. She looked like she was ready to kill anyone that stood in her path.

Even though Joe was relieved at a possible rescue, he

worried that this would turn out worse now that she'd arrived. Irene was clearly in no shape to confront someone as skilled as AB, and he was all but useless tied to a chair. He also wondered what type of drugs she had ingested and how long they'd last.

AB finally broke the silence by chuckling. "I will admit, I am a little impressed at how you managed to find me."

"It's my job to weed out the scum and villainy in London."

"Tenacious *and* dramatic. I do like that."

"Dramatic?" Irene shifted on her feet, inching ever so slightly closer to them. "I'm not the one occupying an entire warehouse to keep one man hostage."

AB ruffled Joe's hair, causing the split in his cheek to sting.

"Oh, but we've had such fun. Haven't we, Doctor? We were just discussing how this whole situation would play out. We both had excellent predictions."

"Let him go. Your quarrel is with me. I'm the one who's been disrupting your plans and putting your men in jail. He is simply my assistant."

"And yet, here you are to rescue him," AB observed flatly.

"I am here for *you*," Irene said, narrowing her eyes.

Joe knew that her words were spoken out of anger, but he couldn't help the small bit of pain that stung his heart.

AB considered her words, then patted him again. "Oh, we're not going to pretend that the good doctor here is an innocent bystander, are we? From what I've observed, if it weren't for him, you wouldn't have solved half the cases you did. No, silly girl, he is very much an important part of you. This is why you dragged yourself here looking – and feeling, no doubt – about the same as a train wreck. Otherwise, you would've waited. I forced your hand by putting this handsome man in danger."

Joe noticed how AB had shifted her words. Just ten minutes ago, he wasn't important to Irene at all, and now he was the thing keeping her together? She was attempting to get a rise, hoping her opponent would make a mistake. Usually, Joe wouldn't worry, but Irene was right on the edge, and any emotional sentence could tip her over.

She moved her eyes away from AB and finally looked at him. Her expression changed from determination to pleading desperation. Her eyes softened, her mouth turned up. It only flashed upon her features for a fraction of a second, but it was enough to light a spark inside Joe.

She was here to rescue him, so he needed to help her any way he could.

Irene appeared to change her tactic, shifting on her feet to a more relaxed pose. The gun never wavered from her primary target, but she looked intrigued as if approaching a new mystery.

"Tell me your story, then. You saw your country turning to chaos and decided to take advantage?"

"My father and two brothers went to war for Hitler," AB told her, giving in to Irene's quizzical gaze. "I saw them do things they wouldn't do in a million years, all for *his* name. It made me wonder what people would do for me, for *my* name, if I gave them enough resources."

"And yet, no one seems to know who you are," Irene retorted.

"It's a figure of speech. The only thing people need to know is what I can do for them. I'll admit that I tried being the perfect Nazi woman, but housework and raising babies weren't for me. So, I branched out and started acquiring connections. There were many opportunities during the war, especially with soldiers. Some of them had their minds toyed with so much that all you had to do was offer them a glimmer of hope and they'd climb on board. Then, my country started losing and I knew I had to move on – out of Germany and to the winning side. My connections came with me, and suddenly, I had a small organization of people with different skill-sets waiting to be sold to the highest bidder."

Irene chuckled darkly. "Consulting criminal."

"Oh, I like that a lot," she purred. "Has a nice ring to it."

Irene laughed again. "I'm not sure if you figured out who my father is, but he became quite famous for his knack for solving mysteries. And for creating enemies. He knew someone like you – an evil man with a similar agenda. You know what my father did to him?"

"Enlighten me."

"He pushed him off a cliff." Irene's words turned foul, and Joe could practically feel the storm clouds brewing above her. "Now, release Joe nicely because the more tired I grow, the more I am inclined to shoot you and go back to bed."

Joe stared at Irene, trying to work out the story she'd just told. He didn't know if it was true or not, but he was willing to bet that her father had, indeed, shoved a man off a cliff.

AB didn't appear to be as taken with her story. Instead, she said, "Come work for me, Irene Holmes."

"Excuse me?"

"I'll release him right now. I will drop this gun and walk out of here if you join me."

Joe closed his eyes for a moment. He was hoping that the

conversation would be over before AB made her offer. Not that he thought Irene might take her up on it, but because she would definitely listen to it out of pure curiosity, and she couldn't afford any more time on her feet. She'd already begun to sway, the drugs in her system wearing off.

"I don't work for criminals," Irene said. "I catch them and put them where they belong."

"Only because you haven't been given a chance to see the other side." AB spoke with the seductive tone she'd attempted to use on Joe. He almost told her not to waste her breath. "I can give you unlimited resources. Pair that with your unlimited brainpower, and you would be unstoppable."

Joe waited for the inevitable laugh and rejection from Irene, but none came. She stared at AB with a look that Joe knew all too well. She was pondering her words, churning them over in her mind.

Just as Joe began to worry, she set her saw and glared.

"I am not a criminal."

"Aren't you?" AB raised a brow. "How did you manage your way in here, past my guards? You *must've* killed them."

Irene was silent, her eyes narrowed. Had she really shot and killed those men outside the warehouse? Or had she simply

243

knocked them out?

When she didn't answer, AB chuckled. "You are not the saint you think you are, my dear."

"I never proclaimed to be a saint."

"You claim to be on the side of the law, yet how many do you break? How many rules do you rewrite to suit your needs? The only reason you work *with* the law is because they allow you the resources to do your job. Other people have those resources too, Miss Holmes, without the limitations of the law." AB stepped around Joe toward her. The gun was still pointed at him, but it wavered. "Think about it, Irene. The things you could do with no one holding you back. Think of the power you'd have."

For another brief moment, Joe worried that Irene might consider this offer out of sheer exhaustion.

"That is the difference between you and me," Irene replied finally. "I do not want power. I want mystery and intrigue, yes, but I do not solve cases for the power play. I solve them because I am good at it. I solve them because, believe it or not, people are happy when I help them."

"You don't think Bernadette and Mr. Barnes will be happy once my plan is complete? That's two people who walk away with everything they want."

"And one person doesn't get to walk away at all," Irene snapped.

"That person wouldn't contribute anything to society anyway. I'm just helping the world along. I am the kind of ruthless that you could only dream of, Irene Holmes. And if you will not consider joining me, then I am done with this conversation."

"You are correct. This conversation is done. Step away from him and get on your knees."

"It doesn't work that way. *I* am the one in control. *I* am the one with the gun pointed at the man you love."

The two women stared at each other, ice in their pupils. Joe looked around the warehouse, wracking his brain for some way out of this situation.

A sudden smirk ran across Irene's face, crinkling her eyes.

"I do have one thing you don't and will never have."

She paused, presumably for dramatic effect, and Joe nearly groaned out loud. Then, he heard a sound in the distance.

Sirens whirring through the air, growing closer.

"I have people who will come to my aid. I have a team of dedicated friends who'll rescue me whenever I am in over my head. You cannot buy that type of loyalty. Now drop the weapon and get on your knees or I will show you that I am capable of ruthlessly removing people from this earth just the same as you."

The sirens grew louder, the whirring cutting through the stillness and tension of the warehouse.

"You took someone that I love," Irene said, voice rising above the noise. "And you hurt him. You will not get away with that."

AB stepped back. Joe saw her breath quicken in panic. She was distracted by the sirens. He needed to act, to help Irene out as best he could.

The German woman let out a frustrated yell and yanked the back of his chair in a rage. He fell backwards, hitting the ground hard.

A gunshot deafened him. Bits of cement hit Joe's head while the ringing persisted. He clamped his eyes shut as his mind whirled, the ringing stirring panic in his body.

Had he been shot? Was he injured? Where was Irene? He wiggled on the ground as the ringing subsided, attempting to free himself from the ropes.

Irene suddenly appeared in front of him, crouching and

touching his face.

"Joe?" She sounded like she was underwater. "You're okay. You weren't shot. I'm going after her."

He tried to speak, but she disappeared. He felt something tug at the rope around him and the bindings loosened.

The room still wobbled, but Joe shook off the restraints and climbed to his feet. He stood in the warehouse, alone. The chair was tipped over, the rope was cut, and Irene and AB were gone.

The back door was open. He headed right for it, stepping out into the cold. AB rushed through the field of tall weeds, heading up the hill. Irene trailed behind her, struggling through the thick, damp grass. She stumbled and fell but regained her footing, attempting to catch up. Beyond them was an automobile at the top of a long hill – the woman's target destination.

Joe started across the field as well, running as fast as he could. AB still had her gun; once she got to the safety of her car, she was bound to use it.

His feet slapped the grass and he nearly fell but kept moving right to Irene. He caught up and tried to grab her, but she jerked out of his reach.

Sure enough, when AB made it to the top of the hill, she turned and fired off two rounds.

Joe leaped forward, tackling Irene, sending them both crashing to the ground. Bullets whizzed over their heads, and Irene struggled against him, but he didn't budge.

She gave one mighty shove and flipped him off before scrambling to her feet.

"Irene!" Joe called.

His cheek stung, and his hearing wasn't quite back yet, but he pushed himself up and continued after her.

AB climbed into the automobile and started the engine. The tires spat up mud and rocks as she took off.

Irene reached the top of the hill within seconds and raised her gun. She fired every round she had left in the revolver by the time Joe climbed up beside her.

AB's car swerved down the road, the back windshield cracked, two holes punctured through it. The car maintained speed, however, and quickly rounded the corner.

Irene kept squeezing the trigger, the gun making small clicking noises as the empty cylinder turned. Tears streamed down her bruised face as her whole body shook from exhaustion. The police sirens had ceased, but now shouts came from down the hill at the warehouse.

"Irene." Joe took the empty gun as she collapsed into his

arms. He fell to the ground, her against him. She clutched his jacket, burying her face into his neck as he sat on the cold, damp ground.

"We have to get her..."

"She's gone. It's time to go home."

Irene pulled away from him, looking up through red, tear-filled eyes. She touched the cut on his cheek.

"You're hurt..."

A smile came over his face, and he let out a soft chuckle.

"It's nothing. I'm fine."

Her breath heated up his face, and she sniffled as a new wave of tears started in her eyes. He kissed her head before pulling her into him again, stroking her hair and holding her as close as he could. His heart thumped against his chest as he tried to catch his breath. He was cold, in pain, and exhausted, but none of that mattered as he held Irene.

All his anger and frustration dissipated. All the thoughts of boundaries and what their friendship meant slid to the wayside as he comforted her. Despite the arguments they'd had, she showed up to save him, and he knew that he would do the same for her, no questions asked.

He heard footsteps beside him. Lestrade dropped to his

knees.

"She's fine," Joe said immediately to ease the inspector's worries who let out a large, exasperated sigh and sat back on his heels. He looked at Joe, and they both exchanged a look of shared relief.

"There are two wounded men at the side of the warehouse and a scared teenager who surrendered immediately. Otherwise, we're clear."

Joe nodded in understanding.

Lestrade stood and shouted orders at his men.

Irene shifted in Joe's lap again, seemingly out of tears, and looked up at him.

"Thank you, Joe," she said, her voice horse and quiet.

He brushed some damp hair from her face and replied softly. "For what?"

"For just... being here... always."

"I wouldn't want to be anywhere else." The wind picked up, and he shivered. "Well, right now, I can think of at least one place I'd rather be."

This got a chuckle out of her, which made him smile.

"Let's go back to Baker Street. I have a feeling Miss Hudson is waiting there with a cup of tea for us."

Chapter XIII

The End of the Year at Baker Street

Four days after the events at the warehouse, Irene and Joe sat across from Mr. Cullens at 221B. His usually polished appearance seemed a big haggard today, the bags under his eyes more prominent. Irene perched on Joe's armrest, unable to hide her furrowed brow and disappointed expression.

"There is no crime you can hold them for?"

Mr. Cullens shook his head, his square jaw clenched in frustration. "Unfortunately not."

He had arrested Bernadette and Mr. Barnes, but without proof that they were involved in a murder scheme, they were released. Irene had argued that she gave them all the evidence they needed. Still, Cullens informed her that while she technically prevented a murder, her testimony would be considered hearsay in a courtroom.

After her release, Bernadette had left the city, heading south – presumably to live with her sister – but was on the watch-list should she ever return to London. Timothy had fired Mr. Barnes and placed a new graduate with a business degree in charge of Aston's Department Store.

Mr. Digby had fled as soon as the shooting began at the warehouse and hadn't been seen or heard from since. Cullens had apologized profusely for bringing Digby into Irene's home, but she had shrugged the incident off, silently praising her instincts for not trusting the man from the start.

Now, Cullens held a folder in his lap that he hadn't addressed yet, and she was eager for him to mention it. Finally, after apologizing again for the injuries both Irene and Joe incurred, he tapped the file with his finger.

"I spent the past few days and one or two sleepless nights scouring my resources and traded in a few favours for this." Irene grabbed the file as soon as he set it down, immediately flipping through the pages.

A few photos of a young woman, barely older than Irene, were stuck to a bare-bones profile.

"Adeline Böhmer," Irene read the name at the top of the page, then skimmed the rest of the information.

"I only managed to find records of her until she left the Woman's League. After that, she doesn't exist."

Joe glanced at the file, his brow furrowing. "I'm curious as to why she would use her own initials to sign her letter."

Cullens answered him with a theory of his own, but Irene interjected before the poor man was finished his sentence.

"Because it doesn't matter if I know it or not. She's a ghost, so even knowing her name doesn't make it easier to find her."

A small photo of Adeline in a uniform slid onto her lap. She glanced at the two men who chatted with one another before she swiped the photo. She gave a flick of her wrist behind the file, and the photo sailed down beside Joe's chair, lost in the pile of books.

She had no idea why she felt the need to keep it, but it was hers. At least until later, when Cullens no doubt noticed it missing.

She closed the file and handed it back. "Thank you for letting us be part of this investigation."

He chuckled and stood. "The choice wasn't entirely mine, Miss Holmes. You certainly have a knack for placing yourself directly into any situation you want."

Irene stood as well, holding out her hand. "The talent comes in handy, I will say that."

"It certainly does." He gave her a playful wink, then turned to Joe. "Good day to you both."

Irene walked him to the hallway, ready to close the door behind him, but he paused, hat in hand, at the top of the stairs.

"Perhaps, Miss Holmes," he began, his white teeth shining in a playful grin. "After the holidays, we might grab a bite to eat. I would love to hear some of your tales and get to know you a little bit better."

Irene was completely blindsided but managed a pleasant smile, ears warming. "Sure. That would be... lovely."

The grin stayed on Cullens face as he stuck his hat on, nodding a final good-bye before heading down the stairs.

Irene watched him leave and felt both intrigued and cautious. The holidays were set to be busy for her and Joe, with both a Christmas and a New Year's party that she kept inviting everyone to. But there was nothing upcoming in the new year.

It would also be beneficial to have a connection in the British government to use whenever she needed a favour or two. Though, the way Mr. Cullens looked at her, she had a feeling he had more than simple friendship on his mind.

She scowled at the empty hallway, then retreated back into

the flat.

Joe tucked their still-full board against the wall next to the tree before turning and noticing Irene's perplexed expression.

"Everything alright?"

"Oh, yes," Irene waved him off. "This case just took its toll on me."

She scooped the photo of Adeline from the floor, tucking it into the drawer in her desk.

Joe continued to stare at the board, then flicked the initials with his finger. "I doubt we'll ever see her again. Even if she made it out of that car, she'd be foolish to show her face in London."

"Foolish indeed," Irene agreed.

Joe sighed. "Well, I'm off. I'll be back for supper."

"Does Sarah know you were kidnapped?"

He shook his head. "We're still working through a few problems regarding my particular career choice, so I've opted to leave that out for now."

"Probably for the best," Irene said, rearranging some angel hair on the tree. "Many people don't understand exactly what our job entails."

"Half of the time, *I* don't understand our job."

255

Irene laughed with him, then watched him get his coat, hat, and gloves. He gave her a wave and left the flat. As soon as he was gone, she grabbed her own hat and coat, a mission at the forefront of her mind.

*   *   *   *   *

Irene strolled through the crowd, breathing in the damp afternoon atmosphere, the shouts of sailors and dockworkers filling the air. Men bustled about, dragging crates and suitcases and various other luggage. Some of it went onto local freight ships, other pieces were loaded onto vessels that would travel across the ocean to North America.

A dockworker spotted Irene and tipped his stained hat at her. "Back again today, Miss?"

Irene nodded but barely glanced at him.

"Must be waiting on someone special for you to come here four days in a row," he grumbled, grabbing some rope and carrying on down the dock.

She continued her search, scanning the crowd. Just as her hopes for today were dashed, her gaze finally landed on a tall woman making her way through the people toward the loading plank of a large freighter. Her hair was tucked up into a dark hat, and she wore flat shoes, but her head met the height of most of the men wandering the docks.

Irene aimed right for her, expecting her adrenaline to rise and her heart to thud in her ears, but she was surprisingly calm as she approached Adeline.

The woman turned and saw her, and for the briefest of moments, panic flashed across her face. She quickly regained her composer and put a sly smile on.

"Irene Holmes," she said, placing her large suitcase in front of her as if shielding herself from an attack Irene might make. "You seem to be healing nicely."

Irene nodded to the suitcase. "I assumed that with your connections, you would have been halfway to America."

Adeline let out a dramatic sigh. "It's hard to find good help these days. Plus, you nicked my shoulder when you took those shots at me. Couldn't very well walk around London injured and bloody; it's not *my* style." She made a point of looking at Irene's cuts and bruises before waving her hand at the ship. "There are better places out there, where my talents would be of better use."

Irene ignored the attempted insult and fished a photo from her coat pocket, holding it tight as the wind blew.

"Do you mind if I keep this?" She held up the photo of Adeline as a young woman. "I like to have insurance that my city will never be disrupted again."

"You found information on me, did you?"

Irene nodded, then gestured to all the people milling about. They ignored the two women, probably assuming they were having a chatty good-bye with each other.

"Shall I say out loud where this picture was taken, Adeline? I think as soon as I name the country where you grew up, you wouldn't make it on that ship." Irene finally saw a hint of worry in the woman's eyes. She smirked and tucked the photo back into her pocket. "I don't feel like inciting a riot at this moment, but I do have a question for you."

Adeline didn't answer, merely raising an eyebrow.

"Why did you sign your note with your actual initials? I assumed because it didn't matter if we knew your true name, but I think there was more of a reason."

"Call it common courtesy. As much as your interference annoyed me, I wanted to show you some sort of respect. And it had been so long since I'd used my own name that it felt freeing in a way."

Irene blinked at her for a moment, knowing exactly where

she was coming. For years, Irene had been reluctant to share her last name with anyone in case they connected her to her father. But now, she wore it with pride.

Adeline sighed. "You came here with a gun. Are you going to shoot me, Irene?"

"That was my intention." She hooked her thumb in her jacket pocket where her uncle's revolver sat, fully loaded. "I didn't even tell my inspector friend where you were because I didn't plan on letting you leave here alive."

The whistle for the boarding sounded behind them. "You'd better get on with it, then."

Irene was tempted to call her bluff and put a hole through her chest right there. Her fingers tightened over the handle of the revolver as she ran through her options quickly in her mind.

If she shot Adeline, then that would end any further potential involvement in anyone else's lives. This woman had hurt Joe and caused pain and death for many other innocent people. If she got on that boat and went to America, nothing would stop her from doing the same schemes over there. True, she would no longer be Irene's problem, but the idea of letting this woman manipulate and hurt any more people didn't sit well with her.

She would get away with shooting Adeline, as well. All

Irene would need to do was hold up the picture of the woman in a Nazi uniform, and the crowd might take her out before Irene even got the chance.

Adeline leaned forward, speaking low and threatening. "I overestimated you sadly. I thought you would have pulled that trigger by now, but perhaps your ruthlessness only goes so far. You may be a problem-solver, but you are no killer. Take your leave, Miss Holmes."

Irene's finger found the trigger, and she pulled the gun from her pocket.

Before she could raise it, however, a dockworker stepped between them, addressing Adeline.

"May I take your bags, Miss? One of the last groups of American soldiers are boarding now. We'd best get you on that ship."

Adeline gave a curt nod to the worker, then glanced quickly at Irene, a smirk on her face. She still held the gun at her side, finger itching to pull the trigger before this despicable woman got away.

"Goodbye, Miss Holmes."

Irene glared, her palms sweaty and adrenaline rushing through her. She did her best to hide her frustration as she

260

moved her finger off of the trigger, pouring all her hate into her final words to Adeline.

"If you ever come back to London, Miss Böhmer, know that I will find you, and I will happily empty this gun into your chest."

Adeline nodded slowly. "I believe that Miss Holmes. Let's hope that day never comes, for both our sakes."

She backed up a few feet before stepping up onto the loading plank. She quickly skirted behind a small group of soldiers, putting a shield between herself and Irene.

She marched up the ramp as confident as ever, though, looking straight ahead, but as Adeline stepped on the boat, Irene caught the worried look over her shoulder. She disappeared onto the deck and into the ship.

Irene blew out a long breath, watching the steam form in front of her in the cold air. The crowd around the ship bustled and yelled to each other, pushing crates and freight up and down. The smell of the metal ships and the damp air from the Thames moved through the wind, surrounding her. As if everything around her came back into focus, she was suddenly very aware that she stood in the middle of a busy dock with a loaded gun in her pocket.

While she waited for the workers to release the ship, anger built up inside her. Had she just let Adeline escape? Or had Irene simply stopped herself from making a decision that didn't belong to her in the first place?

Had her father felt this conflicted before he'd killed *his* nemesis? Did he even have a choice at all or was it merely self-preservation when he'd thrown Moriarty from the cliff?

Irene watched the ship pull away from the harbour, sailing toward the ocean. Perhaps these times were different from when her father was a younger man. The world had been through war again and maybe vigilante justice was not the only option.

It was too late now, anyway.

And Irene wasn't a vigilante. Like Adeline said, she was a problem-solver, not a killer.

As she headed back to Baker Street, though, she made herself a promise that if the woman ever did come back to London, she'd adopt that vigilante title and guarantee Adeline's life end wherever she stood.

*   *   *   *   *

The next day, only three days before Christmas, Irene stared at the tree lit up behind Joe. He peacefully read his book, but she

262

could tell he was restless. He finally put the book down and looked at her.

"Did your father actually push that man off a cliff?"

"Have you not read that far in the stories yet?" Irene retorted, raising a brow.

"Not yet. I recently finished the one about the lady cyclist."

"Well, not to spoil anything for you, but Father did, in fact, push Moriarty off a cliff. Then he faked his own death so that anyone who wanted to harm him would back off. He played dead for three years."

Joe stared at her, his mouth slightly agape, then he let out a loud snort of laughter. "The more I learn about Sherlock Holmes, the more I see where your dramatics come from."

"I am not dramatic," Irene said, a playful smile on her lips.

Miss Hudson entered the room then, tea tray in her hands. Joe stood to help her, grabbing the plates of sandwiches.

"You are, without a doubt, the most dramatic person I know," he replied.

The old woman snorted, nodding in agreement. "That's an understatement."

Irene scowled at both of them, retrieving a sandwich before turning to Miss Hudson. "Do you recall when Father faked his own death?"

The landlady threw her hands in the hair as if exasperated with the situation all over again.

"Good heavens, yes. Broke my poor mother's heart. She used to tell that story and her face would grow red just thinking about it. Then, your father nearly gave her a heart attack when he returned. Not to mention the shock it gave to poor John."

Irene beamed with pride, remembering the glee on her Father's face whenever he'd tell the story and how Uncle John would roll his eyes even though a smile would tug his lips.

"Father disguised himself as a homeless man and walked right into Uncle John's office. When he wasn't looking, Father whipped off his costume and asked for a cigarette. My poor uncle fainted on the spot."

They all laughed, but a sadness drifted over Irene. She longed to see her father smile like that again, and she desperately wanted her uncle to tell more of his stories.

Miss Hudson must've seen her withdrawal because she clasped her hands together, changing the subject.

"I'm glad you kids have cleared up this case. There's been too much excitement for my liking and I am more than ready to settle down for the holidays. Now, eat up."

She left the room, and Joe and Irene finished their sandwiches. Joe set his plate on the tray and sipped at his tea, retrieving his book from the side of his chair.

Meanwhile, Irene stared at him, a debate weighing in her heart. She had yet to disclose to Joe precisely what happened with her father. He knew little snippets, she was sure, but perhaps if she told him the full story, the weight would be lifted from her chest.

"When I was seventeen, my father had a bad fall by the hives on the bee farm," she began, talking before she stopped herself. If she didn't tell the story now, she feared she never would.

At her words, Joe placed his book down and leaned forward in his chair, listening intently.

"He was on a ladder, observing something on the roof of the house. He became suddenly confused as to what he was doing and tried to quickly climb down but slipped and fell. He ended up in the hospital with a twisted ankle and a broken arm that never quite healed right. We had a specialized doctor come and ask me and Uncle John different questions about Father's mental state. He determined that his mind was going quickly. He needed to be watched almost constantly and prevented from doing certain activities deemed dangerous. He couldn't handle things like chemicals or weapons should he get confused and misuse them or harm himself.

"Uncle John, who'd been advising at the university a few days a week, retired and lived with us full-time. I didn't get a job because I couldn't bear the thought of being apart from Father and have something happen. I picked up odd jobs around the small town but was never far away. He went downhill around the start of the war until he would just stay by the fire, occasionally plucking away at his violin. He would sit at the table and eat his meals, then back to the fireplace. He'd ramble on about old cases and get angry at odd things from his past.

"Then, one day, I went to take his violin to clean it, and he grabbed my wrist and told me to put it down. It only lasted a brief moment before he recognized me and burst into tears at what had just happened, but I will never forget that look in his eyes. It broke my heart, Joe. So, I left. I came back to London during a war to run away from my sick father."

Tears fell down her face, and she dropped her head into her hands, completely out of breath and ashamed. She felt Joe sit beside her, wrapping his arm around her shoulders.

"I left him, Joe. I left him, and I haven't been back since. I haven't even written to him. Uncle John came to fetch me a few years ago and died trying to convince me to come back to the farm because I was too damn stubborn and scared. I'm still scared. What if I write to him and he doesn't know the letter is from me?"

"Oh, Irene..." Joe squeezed her tighter, voice soft and soothing. "I'm so sorry. I'm sure he will know. I can help you if you want. We can take as much time as you need."

Irene was silent for a long time, thinking about Joe's offer. Six months ago writing a letter to her father wouldn't have even crossed her mind as she had made all attempts to forget about his condition. But now, sitting on the sofa with Joe, staring at the twinkling Christmas tree, the timing felt right.

"It still terrifies me, though. I hate this feeling. I don't get scared often."

"Everything scares me," Joe admitted, earning a chuckle from her.

"I will admit one thing, though," she said. "I was scared last week, in that warehouse."

"What? You didn't seem scared at all."

"Adeline had a gun to your head and you were bleeding and tied to a chair. I was terrified of something happening to you.

You *weren't* scared?"

"Funny enough, not as much as I should've been, I'm sure. As soon as you showed up, some part of me knew everything would work out. I mean, you looked horrible, but with you there, I figured we would get out of the situation somehow."

Irene sat straight and looked at him. "Perhaps we do make each other better."

"If anything, we bring out the crazy in each other."

She gazed down at her hands, the scabs almost gone from her knuckles. She took a deciding breath and nodded.

"I will write to Father. I think I shall tell him about moving back to Baker Street and our first case together. Perhaps I should write a story like Uncle John did. He would find that funny."

"I think that's a great idea."

Father's chair caught her eye and she stared at the three cushions still piled on the seat.

Joe followed her eyes, then let out a thoughtful grunt.

He wound his fingers into hers and stood, tugging her hand gently. She raised an eyebrow at him but stood. He led her right in front of Father's chair and her heart sped up. She looked at him, and he smiled back at her.

"Perhaps it's time?" His blue eyes were so hopeful, and he

looked longingly at her, desperate to help.

Irene looked back at the chair, tears welling in her eyes. He stood behind her, encouraging her, and put his hands on her shoulders.

"A Holmes is meant to sit there," he said softly into her ear, "and command 221B."

She reached out slowly and gathered the pillows in her arms, clutching them to her chest. The chair's dark fabric held so many memories, and the various chips and nicks in the wooden arms told so many stories.

A tear rolled down her cheek, but she squared her shoulders. She needed to be brave. She needed to move on with her life.

Setting the pillows gently onto the floor, Irene quickly sat in the chair before she could second guess herself.

A wave of familiarity washed over her like a tsunami. For countless nights she'd sat with Father here, going over cases or reading books. Many times, she'd stolen the seat from him, only to be scooped up in his arms and playfully tossed on the couch. She ran her hands over the armrests, feeling every uneven bump in the soft wood.

"It does suit you," Joe observed, beaming down at her, his own eyes wet with tears. "I'm so proud of you, Irene."

"Thank you." The words came out hoarse and quiet, her voice barely above a whisper.

She kicked off her slippers and pulled her legs up, wrapping her knees in a hug. Joe stepped forward and kissed her on the head, then returned to his chair, wiping tears out of his eyes as he went.

Moving on didn't mean forgetting everyone and everything from the past, Irene decided. It meant accepting things as they are now, letting them become a part of you and make you stronger.

*   *   *   *   *

The afternoon sun streamed in through the windows, lighting up 221B on a pleasant Christmas Day. Irene insisted that Miss Hudson and Eddy receive their gifts first, to which no one argued. The woman had opened a basket of vegetable and flower seeds, with Irene and Joe's promise to fix up the back garden so she would have her own space to grow whatever she liked. Irene had also presented her with the tea tray she had stolen from Margaret's Tea House from their last case.

They'd bought Eddy very expensive shoes to match Thom's fashionable footwear and Joe gave him a copy of the photo he'd taken of Irene atop of the brick wall to keep at his desk in his new office.

It was Irene's turn. She ripped the paper off the small wooden box, eager to open whatever present Miss Hudson had gotten her. She opened the lid, revealing brand new chemistry equipment. Vials and bottles shone up at her in the light. She touched them gingerly, a flutter of excitement in her stomach.

"They're university grade," Joe told her. "There are some tools in there that even I've never seen."

Irene wiggled with excitement in her chair by the fireplace, wanting to do every experiment at once. "Oh, thank you, Miss Hudson!"

"Joe helped me out," she admitted.

From his spot beside Miss Hudson, Eddy shook his head. "You know, you're encouraging house fires and potential poisonings."

"So long as she doesn't poison us, Inspector."

Irene set the equipment down carefully by the fire as Joe handed her another gift.

It was a large flat box, wrapped in a lovely ribbon. Joe appeared nervous but nodded at her to open it. She ripped the ribbon and popped the top off.

A deep green gown was folded pristinely inside. She gently took the shoulders and stood, letting the packaging fall to the ground. The sleeves were set off the shoulder, the back plunged low. It looked so familiar…

Irene gasped

"How did you know this is the one I've wanted since the summertime?"

Joe smiled. "I saw you looking at it months ago, during our first case. I thought it odd at the time that someone like you would be eyeing up such a fine garment. Until I got to know you, of course."

Eddy whistled. "We shall have to take you out everywhere and show you off."

Irene raised a brow at him. "I shall take myself out and show myself off. Thank you, Joe. This is beautiful."

She attempted to fold the dress back into the box, but Miss Hudson scowled and took the whole lot from her, opting to do it herself.

In the mean time, Irene clapped her hands together. "I have one more present for Joe. Miss Hudson, would you be so kind?"

The housekeeper secured the lid on the box, then her eyes lit up.

"Oh, yes. I'll be back in a moment."

She hurried away downstairs to her own flat.

Joe looked at Irene. "What did you do?"

"I got you a gift."

Truthfully, two weeks ago, Irene almost cancelled this particular present, thinking that she and Joe were done for good. But they'd mended things, and he'd said numerous times how he looked forward to spring at Baker Street, and they'd chatted in-depth about how to fix up the back garden.

Which meant he was staying.

Miss Hudson entered the room with a large hatbox in her hands, setting it at Joe's feet. He reached down to pull the lid off, and the box jiggled.

He froze. He looked at Irene, who met his excited trepidation with a huge grin.

"Hurry on," she urged.

A small white puppy popped its head out of the box, its pink ears folding back as it looked at Joe, tail wagging.

He reached into the box, scooping the little terrier into his arms. It squirmed in his grasp, licking his chin with its tiny tongue.

He looked at Irene again with tears in his eyes.

"She's mine?"

Irene nodded. "She's nine weeks old. From the old man that we met on our last case. I have several names I like, and I shall run them by you, but it is, of course, your choice."

"Of course." Joe laughed and touched his nose to the pup's. He set her down, and she looked around and let out a small, tough bark before disappearing underneath the chair. Joe immediately dropped to the ground, fishing her out of trouble.

"I don't know if you've given me a pet or simply another Irene to look after."

The pup squirmed and Joe nearly lost hold of her.

Irene leapt from her chair and grabbed the puppy before she fell from his arms. It instantly grabbed her hair, gnawing on it.

"I did choose the perky, rambunctious one. I thought it might be more fun."

Joe beamed at her. "It will be."

*   *   *   *   *

Christmas came and went with food and sleepless nights, everyone taking turns letting the puppy – now christened Isla – outside every couple of hours. Some nights, Joe slept on the couch because Isla couldn't manage the stairs to his bedroom yet.

Soon, everyone gathered at 221B for New Year's Eve.

Irene's new dress sat comfortably on her, tucking in all the right spots. Every time she looked at herself in the mirror, she beamed with pride.

Sipping at her champagne, she surveyed 221B. The sitting room was full of chatter and drinks clinking together. Thom, dressed to the nines, flirted with Madame Jeannie, who somehow towered over him yet made herself seem so delicate in his presence. Sarah, who presumably had forgiven Joe for everything, exchanged recipes with Marla by the Christmas tree, becoming fast friends while Joe and Eddy chatted with Miss Hudson by the fire.

Isla bit at Joe's shoes and he bopped her on the nose several times in the middle of the conversation.

Irene looked past everyone to the window as light snow began to drift down from the sky. The door to the hallway was ajar, so she slipped out of the room and descended the steps, counting each one out of habit.

She stood in the front hall, her nose pressed to the glass while the snow gathered on the pavement and road. It brightened the street, coating everything with a fresh white blanket. Irene stepped out into the chill and watched her breath steam up the air in front of her.

She didn't know how long she had been out there, but she heard Joe's voice from just inside the door.

"Irene?"

She turned on the pavement and held out her hands, catching the snowflakes. "Everything is good now, isn't it, Joe?"

He laughed. "It certainly is."

She looked at him through the white flakes. "London's rebuilding, and so are we."

She didn't know if it was the happiness or the champagne that made her feel philosophical on this particular day, but she looked up at the sky, her eyes closed, enjoying the cold snow on her skin.

"You're turning red. Can we admire London from inside the building?"

He playfully grabbed her arm and tugged her inside.

She stumbled over the threshold, bringing a cold wind with her. As she straightened, Joe kept a soft grip on her arm while he shut the door, presumably worried that she'd trip again. A curl fell into her eyes as she looked up at him and he brushed it away, tucking the hair behind her ear.

His fingertips tingled her skin. For the briefest of moments, her breath caught in her throat. His hand paused against her cheek, gently cupping her face. He stood close enough for her to feel the warmth radiate off of his body, and he looked down at her with a thousand emotions swirling behind his blue eyes. His lips parted slightly as if he were about to speak.

Irene wasn't sure what to do, so she froze, not daring to break whatever moment they were having, wanting to live in this space and time for a while longer. She recalled what Madame Jeannie said about the moments where people knew that they were with someone they were destined to be with forever. While Irene didn't believe in destiny, she felt like this could be one of those moments.

Joe Watson was her best friend and he would stay by her side forever, she was sure.

He pressed his forehead to hers and let out a sigh that she didn't quite understand. He seemed frustrated and held her waist gently but firmly as if he never wanted to let her go.

The tips of their noses touched for the briefest of moments, and Irene's ears warmed. She had no idea what she was supposed to do next, afraid in case it was the wrong move.

Joe broke the moment, and Irene was unsure if she was

relieved or disappointed. He pulled away, seemingly out of breath, giving her a kiss on the forehead.

Movement came from the stairs. Isla hopped down, letting out a small bark with each step she descended.

Joe released Irene and hurried to the puppy, scooping her up.

"What are you doing, you little rascal?" He laughed and brought her to the front hall.

Irene couldn't help the smile that spread over her face as she watched Joe make silly kissing noises to the squirming pup. He looked at her, his eyes crinkling with a smile.

He pulled her into a one-handed hug, the other securing Isla so she wouldn't fall. Irene wrapped her arms around Joe's waist and gave a squeeze.

"Happy New Year, Irene Holmes," he said, grinning down at her.

She reciprocated his smile. "To many more, Joe Watson."

They stared out at Baker Street, with Isla making small growling noises as she tried to chew Irene's hair. Whatever the new 1947 brought to Baker Street, she was excited and ready to take on the challenge. And as she hugged Joe, she knew in her heart that he felt the same way.

THE END OF

COLLECTION ONE

HOLMES & CO. WILL RETURN IN:

COLLECTION TWO

THE ADVENTURES OF HOLMES & CO.

About the Author

 Allison Osborne lives in Ontario, Canada with her son, their West Highland Terrier, and an overwhelming amount of vintage trinkets. She attended the University of Western Ontario for creative writing, and when her mind isn't wandering through 1940s England, she's busy dabbling in scriptwriting and other grand adventures.